FELL

1987 Best Books for Young Adults (ALA)
1987 ALA *Booklist* Books for Youth Editor's Choices
1988 Books for the Teen Age (New York Public Library)

NIGHT KITES

1991 California Young Reader Medal
Best of the Best Books (YA) 1966–1986 (ALA)
1986 Recommended Books for Reluctant Young
Adult Readers (ALA)
Booklist's Best of the '80s

LITTLE LITTLE

1981 Notable Children's Book (ALA)
1981 Best Books for Young Adults (ALA)
1981 *School Library Journal* Best Books of the Year
1981 Golden Kite Award (SCBWI)
1982 Books for the Teen Age (New York Public Library)

GENTLEHANDS

Best of the Best Books (YA) 1966–1992 (ALA)
1978 *School Library Journal* Best Books of the Year
1978 Christopher Award
1978 Outstanding Children's Books of the Year
(The New York Times)
1979 Books for the Teen Age (New York Public Library)

IF I LOVE YOU, AM I TRAPPED FOREVER?

1973 Outstanding Children's Books of the Year
(The New York Times)
1973 Child Study Association's Children's Book of the Year
1973 *Book World*'s Children's Spring Book Festival Honor Book

DINKY HOCKER SHOOTS SMACK!

Best of the Best Books (YA) 1970–1983 (ALA)
1972 Notable Children's Books (ALA)
1972 *School Library Journal* Best Books of the Year
Best Children's Books of 1972 (Library of Congress)

ometimes I tried to imagine myself living in Providencia with Esteban. I knew that was where he wanted to live his life. I didn't know if I could bear to be that far from the United States. When I thought about it, I'd tell myself, *Slow down, Anna B. Put it in the Put It Off file.* But you can't stop yourself from daydreaming, from imagining a future with someone you love, no matter how unlikely it seems. I had never really been in love before. I didn't know what I was willing to risk, or even if I *was* ready to risk at all. Since I'd met Esteban, I didn't think any further ahead than graduation from high school. Now suddenly it began to register what it meant that Esteban was undocumented. I could lose him without doing anything to cause it. One day I could turn around and he'd be gone.

Books *by* M. E. Kerr

YOUR EYES IN STARS
2007 Books for the Teen Age (New York Public Library)

SNAKES DON'T MISS THEIR MOTHERS

SLAP YOUR SIDES
2002 Books for the Teen Age (New York Public Library)
2002 ALA *Booklist* Editors' Choice

WHAT BECAME OF HER
2001 Books for the Teen Age (New York Public Library)

BLOOD ON THE FOREHEAD: WHAT I KNOW ABOUT WRITING
1999 Books for the Teen Age (New York Public Library)

DELIVER US FROM EVIE
1995 Best Books for Young Adults (ALA)
1995 Recommended Books for Reluctant Young
Adult Readers (ALA)
1995 Fanfare Honor List *(The Horn Book)*
1995 Books for the Teen Age (New York Public Library)
1994 *School Library Journal* Best Books of the Year
1994 ALA *Booklist* Books for Youth Editor's Choices
1994 Best Books Honor (Michigan Library Association)

LINGER
1994 Books for the Teen Age (New York Public Library)

FELL DOWN
1991 ALA *Booklist* Books for Youth Editor's Choices
1992 Books for the Teen Age (New York Public Library)

FELL BACK
1990 Edgar Allan Poe Award Finalist
(Mystery Writers of America)
1990 Books for the Teen Age (New York Public Library)

SOMEONE
LIKE
SUMMER

by
M. E. KERR

Los Gatos High School

HARPER TEEN
An Imprint of HarperCollinsPublishers

HarperTeen is an imprint of HarperCollins Publishers.

Someone Like Summer
Copyright © 2007 by M. E. Kerr

Library of Congress Cataloging-in-Publication Data
Kerr, M. E.
Someone like summer / by M. E. Kerr. — 1st ed.
p.   cm.
Summary: An upper-middle-class white girl from Long Island and an immigrant worker from Colombia fall in love despite objections from both their families and their community.
ISBN 978-0-06-114101-0
1. Immigrants—Fiction. 2. Prejudices—Fiction. 3. Fathers and daughters—Fiction. I. Title.
PZ7.K46825 Som 2007   2006021465
[Fic]—dc22   CIP
                                                              AC

Typography by Larissa Lawrynenko
09 10 11 12 13   CG/CW   10 9 8 7 6 5 4 3 2 1

First paperback edition, 2009

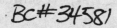

SSC '09

To Renée Cafiero, *sine qua non*,
there from the very beginning of my career
at HarperCollins, with thanks for
so many years of diligence

ONE

THE FIRST TIME I SAW Esteban, he was kicking a soccer ball down a field behind the Accabonac School. His name was on the back of his team shirt. I saw him notice me, smile, then look over his shoulder at me again. I knew he saw me there. I knew he didn't see me a few days later, when I went to hear him sing at Jungle Pete's. Some of the girls at school talked about this singer who appeared there Saturday nights—Esteban Santiago. They said he was hot. Was he!

I went to the soccer field a lot after that. We were well aware of each other, but it was May before we had our first conversation. I'd gone by the field on my bike, after hanging out on the beach with my pal Mitzi and some other kids from school.

I sat on my bike while he was taking a break from the game, lifting his T-shirt up to wipe his brow. Then he saw me, and he strolled over.

"Hello, I'm Esteban Santiago."

"I know who you are."

"How is that?"

"I heard you sing at Jungle Pete's."

"Thank you. For coming. Thank you."

"You're very good," I managed, even though he made me nervous close up.

He asked, "Do you live near here?"

"Very near. I'm Annabel Brown."

"It is good to have you very near." Big smile. His black hair wet from playing.

"Thanks." I could feel myself blushing.

"I have no other fan. My sister comes in her car to watch me. But she doesn't count because we are related." He looked at me with a shy grin. "Yellow is your color, do you know that?"

I had on a sun-colored T and low-rise jeans, boxing sneakers, and yellow socks.

"I know it now," I said.

When I got home I circled the date on my calendar. May 25, 2005.

After that if I showed up when the game was going, he'd find a few minutes to talk with me. I admit I wore something yellow, too, always. We'd flirt.

"You belong in yellow," he'd say.

"You belong back in the game. They're calling you."

"I forget *fútbol* for you." That smile. Away from him I could close my eyes and dream it into my head, and I'd be smiling myself, thinking of him. See, I don't care anymore that he's shorter than I am. It never bothered the girls who went with Tom Cruise. I've fallen in love for the first time, I tell my diary, and lucky me, my diary can't roll its eyes to the heavens and say, *What about Trip Hetherton?*

Fini, dear Diary. I always remember what Dad said about an old heartthrob of his. He said, "Five years later I saw her in an elevator and she was two hundred pounds, eating a chocolate ice cream cone that was all over her face and blouse, grinning at me with her mouth open saying, 'Hey, long time no see.' That's what makes life so great, honey! I once wanted to slash my wrists because she dumped me."

Trip didn't really dump me. I was just never sure of him. One time he'd be e-mailing me and calling me and coming over to watch a movie, another time he'd be so distant that I'd think he'd moved out of town. My brother said it was installment-plan dumping.

That was a whole year ago. I was only sixteen then.

Trip cannot hold a candle to Esteban Santiago.

Can you picture C. Harley Hetherton III strolling out on the small stage at Jungle Pete's, grinning and bowing and then singing until his eyes are shining like stars with his face wet and the crowd going crazy calling out requests? Friends say it happens every Saturday since Esteban started working there.

A day in early June, our first real taste of summer. It was warm even in late afternoon, and some of the players were in shorts.

Esteban wore cargo shorts. He grabbed me by the hand as he came off the field.

"Come with me, Annabel, please," he said. "My older sister wants to meet you."

As we got to the battered red Toyota where Gioconda Santiago puffed on a cigarette, Esteban whispered, "Don't let her intimidate you, Annabel."

Then in a proud tone he said to her, "Gioconda, meet Annabel Brown."

"I've been wanting to meet you," she said. "Last time after the game you ran away."

"I didn't know you wanted to meet me," I said. She had a nice smile. She tapped the long ash off her cigarette on the rolled-down window and introduced me to a girl sitting beside her. Serena something.

Then Gioconda said, "You see my *virgencita* here?" She used her cigarette to point at a china statue of the Virgin Mary on the dashboard. One of those plastic nodding dogs was next to it.

"Yes, I see."

"I pray to it," she said.

"Well, good. Good." I was embarrassed. My family may pray, but we don't talk about it.

"I drive along praying," said Esteban's sister.

I couldn't think of anything to say to that, and it turned out that I didn't have to answer because her next sentence came rolling off her tongue, with a different kind of smile that made her eyes crinkle and her mouth tip slyly to one side. "You are a flour face," she said.

"Thank you." I thought she'd said *flower*.

Esteban was bending over to tie his shoe.

"I pray that Esteban will tell you to stop chasing after him!" she said. This time Esteban heard her, just as I realized she didn't mean a flower. She meant *flour*. White.

"Come on, Annabel." Esteban grabbed my arm and pulled me. *"Vamos!"* We could hear the girls in the car laughing. Esteban said, "When will I learn that I cannot trust her to behave herself? I am sorry. I did not know she would do that."

His sister was not finished. She shouted over her shoulder, "Stop throwing yourself at my brother, Flour Face." Then she said something to Esteban in Spanish. I'd had only two years of Spanish, and I didn't understand it unless the speaker went very slowly. Esteban had to tell me what she'd shouted after me.

She'd said, "The Santiagos don't want any white babies running around, Esteban."

I tried to be cool when he told me his sister said that. I smiled down at his brown eyes and said, "She's rushing things, isn't she?"

"Yes. But she knows I like you . . . that way, Annabel."

"Do you tell her that?"

"She is my family. I do not have to tell her. She sees me looking at you when I am playing."

"Dear old family," I said. "Try to put anything over on them." I hardly heard myself. I kept thinking about what he'd said, that he liked me "that way."

Esteban said, "Years ago there was trouble in my country and my father was captured. We never saw him after. Ever since, my sister protects me too much. I tell her those things don't happen in this country. She still looks out for me always."

"I am sorry about your father, Esteban."

"Thank you. . . . I tell Gioconda don't worry about me. I can take care of myself."

"What does your sister think you're going to do?"

"She is more concerned with what *you* are going to do. Maybe you will take me away from my family, from my country. Do you think you will do that, Annabel?" He smiled. His eyes crinkled, too, but in a sweet way. He was so great-looking. His hair shone like new coal.

"I have something to tell you, Annabel," he said. He took my hand as we walked along. "I am going to do some work for your father."

"What?"

"A week from this Friday afternoon I am going to put the new roof on your garage. Dario Lopez from our house was scheduled, but he has to take a driver's test to get his license."

"And my father hired you?" All the other Latinos who worked for Dad seemed older. Esteban was just twenty. He had no training in construction. Dad never went down to the railroad station, where the unemployed, unskilled immigrants waited for jobs. He had regular crews. He was a major taskmaster.

"Your father hired Dario, but I will take his place."

"I thought you said you cooked at the Pantigo Deli, Esteban?"

"I do. I do all things. I cook. I do yard work. I sing."

I couldn't see him working with Dad's crew. Dad never let them listen to radios while they worked. Other contractors didn't care, but Dad wouldn't allow it. They didn't talk. They just hammered away, putting up house frames in a day, roofs in half a day. They were hard, hard workers!

"My father is a perfectionist, Esteban. Since when are you a carpenter?"

"Since I said I would do it for Dario." He gave me a big smile.

TWO

M Y FATHER'S WORK crews eventually became all Latino. They work for ten dollars an hour.

When my brother was home from Cornell, he was always after Dad. "You call yourself a contractor? You hire slave laborers, Dad. And what happened to the local men you used to hire?"

"The locals want twenty-five, thirty an hour. Some jobs these guys do, the locals won't do."

"So you hire desperate immigrants who'll

work for anything!"

"It's a darn good deal for them," my father said defensively. "Most of them don't speak English, and some don't even have papers. I don't ask questions. I give them steady work. They learn on the job, some of them, and they can earn as high as three hundred a week."

"I can't discuss it with you, Dad. Your mind is made up."

"You college boys don't know zilch about the working world," said Kenneth Brown to Kenyon Brown. "The only thing you really know how to do is spend money someone else earns."

"I waited tables all last summer, Dad, in case you don't remember."

"Oh, is that a job? Do you have any calluses? Is your neck sunburned? If you want to know what work is, watch these Latinos. They're a whole new breed, Kenyon! We've never had people like them! They sock away three fourths of what they earn. They send it to their families."

"So did the Irish when they used to come here summers."

"The Irish never stuck around more than a few months. They were all kids, just here for the summer. Give me the *muchachos* any day! They're the best thing that ever happened out here."

"Out here" is the tip of Long Island, the Hamptons, Seaview to be exact. We were a resort town in the summer, yet more and more people were staying with us longer, and more vacationers were buying houses too. Some said the computer had changed everything—that now people could do their work from home, no need to go into the office every day. Whatever the reason was, we were growing fast, and the new immigrants were a big part of the picture. They did not come to us for a vacation, as so many did. They came here to work.

They came from everywhere: from Brazil, Cuba, Mexico, Colombia, Puerto Rico, Guyana, you name it.

They have changed a lot of things about Seaview. In the supermarkets like Waldbaum's and the IGA, now there were green plantains, yucca, calabaza, and batata. The little delis popping up along Montauk Highway featured *arroz con pollo*, enchiladas, tacos, and tamales. Many church sermon boards were in Spanish and English, and so were some town meetings.

Out in a section of town called Accabonac, where we lived, the biggest problem was finding a place to build sports fields for them. They are soccer players. They all seem to be. That first time I saw Esteban, kicking a soccer ball around a field, the police arrived to warn them all games are supposed to end by six P.M. But sometimes I hear them there at nine or ten, still going, until neighbors call the police back.

Nobody wants soccer fields in his backyard. Last summer my father was one of the few people in our neighborhood who spoke up for the fields when they wanted to put some a few blocks from where they play now. The vote went against the soccer players, and supposedly the town is clearing land near the dump for them. Meanwhile they remain.

"What is the matter with people?" my father said. "We have our golf courses and our tennis courts, our baseball diamonds and our football fields. But we just can't take the idea of having good clean fun going on in our neighborhood if the sport is soccer. We all know who the soccer players are—Latinos!"

"That's not why," my brother argued. "Don't make a race thing out of it. People don't want the noise in their backyards. They don't want the lights at night or the public restrooms!"

"People should be glad the *muchachos* want to recreate in their spare time," said my father. "You don't see them crawling in windows to rob, or hanging around the parking lots to smoke dope and key cars."

There was a fair chance that my father would like Esteban. He admired hard workers because he was one himself. He did not take to Trip. Summers all Trip did was surf and sail, because his family was rich. Trip's big faux pas was to honk the horn for me the night of our first date. My father made me sit in the living room until

Trip figured out he had to get out of his Lexus and come into our house to meet my father. Dad also examined Trip's driving license and told Trip he was to have me back home by eleven thirty P.M.

Our garage hasn't had a car in it for years. Kenyon slept on a pullout bed in my dad's office. Dad's office spilled over into the garage, where Kenyon kept a battered old motorboat, skis, a skateboard, surfboard, all his playthings and gear. Being the only daughter, I always had my own room.

Now, with Kenyon finishing his last year at Cornell, Dad was reclaiming that part of our house. Kenyon was planning to work for Dr. Annan, at Seaview Vet. Someone had to be on the premises overnight with the animals, so a small apartment went with the deal. Charlie Annan was on the zoning board, and he was a trustee of everything from the hospital to the library. Everyone admired Charlie.

Of all things, Dad was creating a screening

room in the garage. I believe this was part of his plan to begin dating again, or as he put it, "to find the right woman for my old age." He said he knew he would never find someone like my mother. He used to say Mom was his university, that she had taught him "culture," that he had not had an original thought in his head for twenty-two years until he married her. He would tell Kenyon and me that he had wanted to name Kenyon Kenneth Brown Junior, and me Mary Brown, after his grandma. But my mother had taught him how important names were, and that if you had an ordinary last name, you deserved an exotic first name.

In our living room was a sampler my mom had made that said: *My heart is free, my head unbowed, I do not join the foolish crowd.*

My father had gotten one of his crews together to install in the garage a hardwood floor and new windows with shutters. He had gotten a permit for a bathroom, a stove, and a sink. He bought a wide-screen TV, a projector, DVD, the works.

Then came all new furniture: two leather chairs that reclined, a leather couch that could convert to a double bed. Thick rugs. Fancy recessed lighting. A white marble-top coffee table that swiveled up to a full-size dining table. My father had learned a lot working for the movie moguls and investment bankers who flocked to our shores summers and weekends. This screening room didn't look like it belonged with the rest of the house. Even my brother was shy about using it for any reason when he was home from college. He kept some of his summer clothes in my bottom bureau drawer. I wasn't surprised to find a few packages of condoms under his swim trunks.

THREE

"Esteban Santiago told me he's going to do the screening room roof a week from Friday," I said to Dad at dinner that night.

"When Dario can't work, Ramón does. Where's Ramón?"

"I don't know anyone named Ramón."

"How did you know Santiago is taking Dario's place, and how do you know him?" Dad asked.

"I've heard him sing at Jungle Pete's. He's fabulous!" I didn't want to admit I went by the soccer field early Wednesday evenings to see him play and to have time with him.

Dad knew I wasn't interested in sports of any kind. Ease into this, I told myself.

Dad said, "Do you talk to this *muchacho*?"

"Not much."

"What do you two have to talk about?"

"I've seen him play soccer. I told him he was good."

"Since when do you care about soccer?"

"I don't care that much about it." I should have said I care about it when Esteban plays, but I didn't really know how to tell my father I might be falling in love with someone I didn't know very much about. I would never be able to answer Dad's usual questions: What does his father do? Where do they live? What does this young man want to do with his life?

All right—I would leave out the love part. Call it a crush. That made less of my feelings, but Dad could live with a crush. Mention love, and Dad gets that lost look in his eyes that says he wishes Mom was alive. Mom would know how to get me through it, or over it, or whatever it takes to get me back on track without any damage.

Dad said, "I don't think you care about soccer at all, Annabel. And I hope you don't care about something else. Someone else."

"Why would you think that?"

"You brought up his name. People can't stop saying the name when they're interested in someone."

I kept eating the meat loaf I'd made using Mom's recipe. I was getting to be a fair cook. I ate and told myself to drop the subject right now.

Finally, Dad said, "So this *muchacho* sings and he plays soccer and now he's going to become a carpenter?"

"Don't call him a *muchacho*, Dad."

"Why not? That's what he is."

I didn't argue the point. It was too hard to explain to my father that calling Esteban a *muchacho* was somehow belittling. Dad didn't get that sort of thing. He called women "gals" and Asians "Orientals." Once I heard him talking to a new Latino crew. At the end of his spiel, he said, "That's it—cha cha cha."

"Great meat loaf, honey!" Dad said. He put down his fork and said, "I hope this *muchacho* will finish that roof up in an afternoon. I'm having a little lunch and matinee that Saturday for a lady friend. I want to impress her. I'm making my spaghetti and she's bringing the movie. I told her I like everything, so when you meet her, don't tell her I only watch war pictures and westerns."

"Who is this mystery lady?"

"Her name is Larkin."

"Larkin what?"

"Just Larkin. She's an artist." He pronounced it *arteest*, his idea of humor. "She only uses one name."

"Like Madonna, hmmm?"

"No, not like Madonna. This woman has a head on her shoulders and she's a serious artist. You should see her place!"

"What's it like?"

"It looks like something out of a magazine. I don't mean *Family Circle*. I mean a high-class magazine like *Architect's Digest*."

"*Architectural Digest*, Dad."

"Yeah, that magazine. Pictures of big shots' homes sort of thing. You know?"

"That's great, Dad."

"She's got class, you know? I'm not talking about money, either. I'm talking about what your mother was always talking about. Originality. I see things a whole new way because of Larkin. She's teaching me how to be chic."

"Dad? That's pronounced *sheek*, not *chick*."

FOUR

MY COUSIN CLAIRE from Maine was visiting us for the weekend, and naturally I suggested Jungle Pete's for dinner. We took my good friend Mitzi Graney with us. She spoke Spanish fluently and dated a Latino guitarist there. The three of us sat at a side table, craning our necks to see the small stage.

Jungle Pete's was this homey little restaurant with terra-cotta walls, exposed brick, and wooden booths, but on Saturday nights it went

Latino, pulsing with light and sound. It balanced live rock acts with Latin pop, and every Saturday Esteban sang with the lead guitarist. He was beginning to get a real following, although as the nights got later, the pint-sized dance floor became more bump than bumps and grinds, and too loud to hear anything but the thumping rock, reggae, and salsa rhythms.

One song he sang made everyone stop and listen. It was called "*Los Niños de Nuestro Olvido*." It was about a little boy from a South American city dreaming of a warm home while he was sniffing glue and living in the street.

"Where did that come from?" Claire said while everyone clapped and whistled.

"The heart," I said. "Did he have tears in his eyes?"

"Hard to tell, he's sweating so," Mitzi said. "He's from the same house as my Virgil. Did I say *my* Virgil? Lately he's dissing me a lot, whatever that's about."

It was a little after ten by the time Esteban came over to our table carrying a thick Cuban sandwich, asking if he could sit with us. I had to be home by eleven thirty Saturday nights, a fact my cousin Claire and Mitzi both knew. What made it possible for me to spend time alone with Esteban was Trip Hetherton, of all people. He had met my cousin many times, and we had even spent a few days at her home in Bangor. Just as Esteban arrived at our table, so did Mitzi's boyfriend, Virgil, who whisked her off to dance. While Esteban sat beside me—the pair of us talking and laughing—Trip asked Claire if she'd try to neotango with him. He knew she was a great dancer, like he was. Suddenly I was alone with Esteban.

"I'm glad you came early enough to hear me sing a little."

"So am I," I said. "I was afraid you didn't see us back here."

"When you come in a room, I can feel you are there."

I laughed, and he shook his finger at me and said, "I am serious, Anna."

Nobody but my family had ever shortened my name. I would have told anyone who did it not to. My mother had named me after a famous poem by Edgar Allan Poe—"Annabel Lee."

But I liked the sound of Esteban saying Anna, and I couldn't speak right away, anyway.

"I am sorry to eat in front of you. May I order something for you? Some *tapas*?"

"We ate a big dinner, but thank you."

"May I take you home?"

"My father wants me in by eleven thirty."

"Then maybe I will see you Friday, when I do roof work."

I didn't tell him I wasn't allowed to ride in a car at night with a boy Dad didn't know. "Yes, maybe we will see each other then. Do you stay here until closing?" I asked him.

"*Sí*, I have to remain until three. When the crowd is less and there is little dancing, I sing again."

"You're very good, Esteban."

"What was it you liked that I sang?"

"'*Los Niños*'?"

"'*Los Niños de Nuestro Olvido*.' Yes, everyone

likes that. It really belongs to the singer Mercedes Sosa. She made it famous."

"I don't know her. I also liked 'Atrevete a'— 'Atrevete'—"

"'Atrevete a Olividarme.' Sí! That song is from the Diva of Salsa. You know Brenda K. Starr?"

"No. I don't even know what the words say. But I've heard you sing it before."

"Every time I sing it now, I will sing it to you, whether you are in the room or not. It becomes our song, Anna."

"Shouldn't I know what it says?"

"I thought you studied Spanish in school?"

"I did, Esteban, but only two years. Not enough."

I could see Trip and Claire coming back to the table.

"This is what it says," Esteban said. "'Dare to Forget Me.'"

Next, Trip stuck out his hand and told Esteban his name.

"How do you do, Trip? My name is Esteban Santiago."

"A true Latino," Trip said. "I thought so when you sang."

"A true Colombian," Esteban corrected him.

"I've been to Mexico," said Trip, "but not to Colombia. Unless you're talking about the university." Trip's idea of humor.

Then they sat down with us, so we had to sit touching. Esteban took my hand under the table. I felt as though we were wired, as though there was electricity we were breathing out, as though we could be on fire any second. The music became very loud, and we couldn't have said anything the other would hear. When I looked across at Claire, she gave me this look, as though she was trying to ask, "What's going on? Since when do you know him?"

I'd remembered what Dad had said about having to say someone's name if you were interested in him, so I hadn't told Mitzi or Claire anything about Esteban. It was too soon.

Trip called the waiter over and said he'd like a *cerveza azul*. I knew they wouldn't proof him there. Claire was twenty-two and didn't need proof.

"What is a *cerveza azul*?" she asked Trip.

"Did I say it right?" Trip asked Esteban.

"I don't know it."

All three had to shout to be heard.

Trip shouted, "I thought that's what you people drank. It has beer mixed with blue curaçao and vodka."

Esteban shrugged.

"I guess I'm going to have to drive *you* home, too," Claire yelled back at Trip, just as the music stopped.

"Thanks but no thanks, Claire." Then Trip looked at me and said in this condescending tone, "Does Daddy still make you be home by eleven thirty? That used to drive me bananas."

Before I left that night, Esteban asked me if Trip had been my boyfriend.

"Yes."

"Were you very serious?"

"No." I didn't say that I was and Trip wasn't.

Esteban said, "I cannot think of you with another. How long were you his sweetheart?"

"Esteban, it wasn't serious."

"Really not?"

"Really not." I liked the fact he was jealous. Already.

When my brother called home Sunday morning, Dad was at the Unitarian church with Larkin. Dad told me he was thinking of leaving the Presbyterian Church and becoming a Unitarian because their thinking was freer. Dad leaving the Presbyterian Church was like me leaving the Girl Scouts. I'd gone to exactly two meetings.

Dad said, "Larkin has given me new eyes. Just for example, Annabel, I never looked at trees before. I never looked at the ocean. I mean really looked."

On the phone Kenyon complained about the war in Iraq, Bush, the subjects he had to soft-pedal around Dad. I told him Dad was chang-ing—maybe not about those things, but he did have a woman who thought the way we did. "Her name is Larkin," I said, "and he's falling in love with her, Kenyon." We talked about the idea that men who were in good, long marriages often remarried quicker than men who weren't. Now, after four years, Dad was sounding like he'd found someone. I think both Kenyon and I were delighted. Then I rushed to tell Kenyon about Esteban. I was sure that Esteban felt the same way I did. He'd kept asking me how serious I had been with Trip, and I'd kept teasing him about being jealous. I'd never even come close to feeling about Trip as I did about Esteban.

"You haven't kissed or anything?" Kenyon asked.

"We've held hands. We're very new. Don't laugh."

"I'm not laughing. How could you fall for someone so fast?"

"Maybe it's pheromones. I remember in health Mrs. Cohen said that males and females emit pheromones that are irresistible to each other."

"I think she was talking about animals, not people."

"She was talking about both, Kenyon. I'd pack my bags and run away with him tomorrow if he asked me." That was what my mom would call hyperbole.

"Well, if he asks you, ask him where he plans to take you. I remember Trip teasing you once about his plans to live permanently on a boat someday . . . in the Florida Keys."

"A yacht, Kenyon, not a boat. Trip's family moors this yacht in Sag Harbor that's a block long."

"But at least you can speak the language in Florida," Kenyon said. "With this new fellow you might end up in Bogotá, which is a lot of city for a small-town girl to handle."

"Maybe I need a big place like Bogotá. Dad says we all need to open our minds to new things."

"Sure we do, cha cha cha," said Kenyon.

FIVE

I LOVED THE WAY ESTEBAN looked that Friday. He had a brown-and-white bandanna around his forehead, which matched his light-brown eyes. He called it a *pañuelo*. His skin was smooth and coffee colored, but you could see where his mustache would be if he hadn't shaved, and his teeth were white with one on the upper right side slightly crooked. I saw a lot of his teeth because he couldn't stop smiling. Neither could I.

My father had a job out in Montauk, so he

was hurrying; but as he was walking down the driveway to his truck, he shouted, "Annabel, this boy doesn't need you around while he works. . . . I'm having dinner with Larkin, so no need to cook for me. I'll be very late."

As soon as he backed his truck out, Esteban came down the ladder and said, "You hear him? He won't be here for dinner. I will be, if you want to have a special paella. Anna, don't touch me yet." I was heading toward him. "Stay away from me and I will tell you why."

"Why?"

"I want to do this job well. I am proud like your father. I am a perfectionist. Remember you told me he is one?"

"Yes."

"I am one too. I do not want a distraction, which is what you are, because you have such soft eyes, I ache. Your father will be gone for dinner. My uncle works at the Pantigo Deli, where sometimes I cook with him. He makes the best paella. I will drive there later and bring some back. We will have a celebration feast that

I have finished my job!"

"We can have it in the screening room," I said. "We can watch a movie."

"*Sí! Sí!* I like that idea. I feel good with you, Anna."

"I do too, with you."

It was hours before I heard him at the door. I called for him to come in. I had decided to make a chocolate cake for our dessert. I was wiping my hands on a dish towel I'd tucked into my jeans as an apron, when he came up behind me.

We couldn't help ourselves. We were hanging on each other and kissing, but Esteban slammed his fist down on the kitchen table and said, "*Basta!* It is almost dark. I have only a little more to do, but I need more nails. I will run and get them, Anna, and you can come with me and get the paella. Then we will be all set for a party after work."

Before he went to the hardware store to get the nails, Esteban introduced me to his uncle, at the deli next door. He asked him to give us extra mussels for the paella.

A voice said, "She doesn't need extra mussels, Esteban. She's muscled her way in very well, hah?"

It was Gioconda, of course, with her mean mouth and her crinkly eyes. What was said next was in Spanish, was angry, both pairs of Santiago eyes flashing. Gioconda pointed at me, her long nails blood-red daggers. Esteban made a fist and held it up to her face as though he would punch her, but she didn't flinch. He finally let his arm drop, shaking his head as though he couldn't believe the things she would do. She marched out the door and he stomped after her, calling over his shoulder to his uncle to make two good paella plates to go.

"Slow down, Esteban," I said as we drove back. His old 80s Pontiac kicked up dust along the highway.

"I am sorry you have to see me so angry, *amante*," he said. "Gioconda makes me undignified. Now that we are away from home, she bosses me as though she is *mi madre*."

All I really heard was "amante." A first. I remembered that from Spanish II. I watched him in profile. I thought of the two songs I liked that he sang at Jungle Pete's. The one about the needy street kid reminded me vaguely of my dad. Every Christmas he collected money from Seaview merchants for toys he'd give to poor kids. His orders were: *No clothes, nothing that is good for the child, just playthings so this little boy or girl will know what our kids find under the tree.* I hoped Esteban had a caring nature, too. That was as sexy to me as the other song he sang: "Dare to Forget Me."

"I don't care if you're undignified," I said.

"But I care! In my life at this time, I have only my pride and my dignity. They are everything."

SIX

"**D**ONE!" ESTEBAN called in to me.

I put the outside lights on so we could see, but it was already too dark.

"It is just a roof," said Esteban. "Nothing much to see. It was not hard. You know, Anna, if I become a carpenter, I will have real money for a change."

I felt like saying, *Not if you work for my father*. He paid apprentices eight dollars an hour and his regulars ten. But Esteban wouldn't have to work for him long. He could go into business for himself after he learned everything. He could become a contractor.

"Don't you want to be a singer, though, Esteban?"

"I am no Juanes. I'd like to write music too, but you need learning. You need it for everything, and I don't have it."

"Who is Juanes?"

"You don't know him? He won one of your Grammys one year for a song called 'A Dios Le Pido . . .' But my making songs and my singing is a dream. I work for tips at Jungle Pete's. That's why I work there only one night. A lot of customers don't tip at all. Hey, let's go in. The mosquitoes are biting."

I made Esteban lie down on the leather couch while I warmed up the paella in Dad's new kitchen. Esteban's uncle had given us extra mussels and even pieces of lobster mixed in with the chicken and rice. I didn't want Esteban to do anything. I swiveled the table up and put a cloth on it with candles in star-shaped holders. Dad had been over to Pier One and bought little extras: lilac soap for the bathroom, salt and pepper shakers in the shape of swans, white napkins with tiny gold swans on them, even a swan vase he had put fresh daisies in.

I put down our best dishes, white ones with gold stars in the middle. Mom had found them years ago on eBay. We hardly ever used them. But I noticed Dad had moved them from the house to the screening room.

I poured cold green tea into tall clear glasses, remembering Dad's new notion (or Larkin's) that you should always be able to see the color of your drink. He announced that he would never again drink his nightly scotch on the rocks in a red glass. He put all our colored glasses into a box for the yard sale he said we would have one day.

I called Esteban's name, but he had fallen asleep. I went over and tickled his face lightly with the corner of a cloth napkin. (No more paper napkins was another rule Dad made since hanging out with Larkin.) Esteban didn't budge.

I played with the gold medal he always wore

41

on the gold chain around his neck. He called it his Santa Cecilia medal. He said she was the patron saint of musicians.

"Hey, you," I said softly, and I squeezed in beside him. "Dinner's ready, Swan Man," I cooed. That name for him just popped out.

Esteban opened his eyes. He was blinking and grimacing. I ran my finger across his brow.

"Anna? Turn off the overhead light, please?"

"Yes, and I want to light candles for us, too."

"Not yet," he said. He sat up and looked into my eyes very solemnly. "I like what you just called me. Swan."

"Do you know that swans mate forever?"

"We are swans then," he said. I felt his small hands touch me.

"Our dinner will get—" but "cold" never came out of my mouth. What happened next came spontaneously and suddenly, like a lighted match touching fireworks. Later I believed that I had known nothing about my own body before Esteban. With Trip, kissing was never so exciting. I liked more being seen places with him. But what I felt with Esteban made me realize all I heard about love in songs, all I saw in movies and on TV, was true. Finally romance was real and there was more to life. It was like discovering a new color or a new taste.

How long was it before Esteban whispered, "No, Anna, no"?

I knew what he meant. We would never control ourselves if we didn't stop as soon as he found the words. It was not the time, not the place, but in all honesty those were the only things that made me agree with him.

I was shaking when I stood up, trembling all the way across the room to the light switch. Even my voice sounded like someone else's when I managed to say, "I'll light candles for us. We want to have dinner by candlelight."

I was looking for matches when I heard Esteban exclaim, *"Condenación! Dios!"*

"What? What?"

Esteban was sitting up on the couch, staring at the ceiling.

I looked up, too. There were rows and rows of

nails coming through the wood on one side.

Esteban was holding his head with his hands.

It took him a few seconds to say, "I was angry with Gioconda when I left you in the deli and went to the hardware store. I got the wrong size nails. They are too long. Oh, Anna, I have made a terrible mistake! How can I ever face your father?"

I didn't know how he could face Dad either. It was too dark out for him to fix it, and he didn't have the right size nails anyway. "Don't worry," I said, "it will—"

He didn't let me finish. He stood up and glared at me. There was this tiny vein pulsing in his forehead.

He said, "Don't lie!" His hands were balled to tiny fists. "It is my bad and I take responsibility for it! You think I can ever face him again? I cannot!"

I wanted to say, Well, don't blame me. Don't look at me with your eyes furious. But more than anything I wanted to put my arms around him, to make everything all right.

"Get away!" he shouted. "Ramón is right! You

girls don't really care about us. You belong with your own!"

"What do you mean? Who's this Ramón?"

"I mean how important this was to me, to do this job well! I told you all I have is my good name and now it is what you say—mud!"

"Who is Ramón?"

"My homie. He guides me."

"He guides you wrong, Esteban. I care a lot about you! Your name isn't mud just because of a little mistake."

"Your father will think it is."

"It's just a little mistake," I repeated, but I didn't sound convincing even to myself.

He gave me the dirtiest look anyone has ever given me, and he spat out the words, very slowly: "You don't know anything!"

But right behind the brown of his eyes were the beginnings of tears.

I just stood there and watched Esteban pick up his tool belt and march out the door. Soon I heard his car start, the wheels skidding down the driveway.

SEVEN

SATURDAY MORNING.

"Larkin?" I said as she stood in the doorway. "Are you Larkin?" I had almost mistaken her for Esteban, her hair was so short and dark.

"And you must be Annabel."

"Come in. My father should be right back."

"I was so sure he said to come at noon."

"He did. Please come in. Something came up he had to attend to."

"Nothing serious, I hope."

"Oh no. Nothing serious."

My father was a wreck. He had come in late last night, so he had not seen the ceiling until this morning. I'd told him how Esteban had left practically in tears, that he was ashamed of what he'd done. I said he wouldn't even eat some food I'd ordered from the Pantigo Deli. I often bought takeout for two even when I was alone, because of the delivery charge, and because I could always eat leftovers.

"Since when does one of my workers get invited to dinner?"

"I just felt so sorry for him, Dad."

"Wait till you see him when I'm finished with him!"

Last night I had put away the tablecloth, the swan salt and pepper shakers, the candles, our good dishes, everything that spelled out romance. All morning I had tried to reach Esteban on his cell phone. He always answered it; he was always looking for work. But that morning there was just his recorded voice.

Larkin walked by me, and I knew instantly she had style and grace: the long yellow skirt with the white high-heeled sandals, the low-cut orange top, the tiny gold earrings, no other jewelry. She seemed to glide past me.

My father has a unique way of showing rage. Not anger—rage. He gets quiet. He speaks in a low tone, so often you have to lean forward to hear him, as though you were slightly deaf. He even gives you these quick little smiles when he says things like "I told that kid how important this job was!"

"He knew it was, Dad."

"How could he be so sloppy?"

"He felt ashamed, Dad, so ashamed."

"He should have."

Quick little smile.

He said, "I'm going down to that house where they all live."

I realized I had no idea where Esteban lived, or who "they" were. Gioconda, I thought, and hadn't he mentioned some man named Dario, someone who had to take a driving test?

My father said, "Be welcoming to Larkin, Annabel. If that boy calls, tell him to get his butt over here on the double!"

"You could serve Larkin paella," I said. "You know I always order too much."

"I don't eat Latino crap!" he snarled.

In fact he loved all of it, particularly paella.

"I don't mind that your father's late," Larkin said.

"He really isn't late. There was an emergency."

"That will give us time to get acquainted, Annabel. I love that name. There was a poem by Poe about a great love between two very young people. 'I was a child and she was a child—'"

"'In our kingdom by the sea,'" I continued the poem.

"Yes. That's it. Her name was Annabel Lee."

"I was named for her. It was my mother's favorite poem."

"Mine too," Larkin said.

You'd turn around on the street if you passed

her, just to get another glimpse. She was not really beautiful, but my father was right: She was different, almost exotic, and she exuded warmth as she strolled around looking things over, speaking to me in this low, sexy voice.

"Would you like a drink, Larkin? I'm sure my father will be right back."

"Oh no, thank you. If I drink in the daytime, I get sleepy."

So much for the bottle of French Champagne my father had put in the refrigerator a week ago.

Larkin handed me a tape. *Backstage at the Kirov*. "This is a documentary about Leningrad's Kirov ballet. I'm a balletomane. Your father tells me he is too."

"Whatever" was all I could say. I'd never heard the word before, but it was easy to figure out what it meant. The idea of my father saying he was a balletomane boggled the mind. Ballet? Dad?

"Are you going to join us for lunch?" Larkin asked.

"No. I think my boyfriend, Esteban, is coming

by soon. I hope so, anyway. He has business with my father."

"Too bad. I hear your dad's spaghetti sauce is superb!"

"Or you could have paella. There's paella, too."

"I'm going to leave the menu up to Kenny."

Kenny? Who had ever called Dad Kenny? He was definitely not a Kenny.

Larkin said, "Will I meet your boyfriend?"

"I wish you would," I said. "Oh, and please don't say he's my boyfriend. My dad might not think he is. I don't even know him that well."

"Your secret is safe with me, Annabel."

Before my father had slammed out the door, he had predicted that Esteban would hide out somewhere. That's what "they" did when "they" made mistakes.

"I don't blame him," my father had said. "What's he going to come back here for? To get hell from me? To hear me tell him he's not getting one red cent until he repairs that roof, and then he's only getting half of what I would have paid him? He's ruined my plans, damn him!

Why would he come back?"

I'd said, "Maybe he'll come back because of me."

"Why because of you?" Then he got it. He just shook his head as though he was really sorry for me. "Honey, these *muchachos*, excuse me, these boys aren't anything like your Trip Hetherton."

"He's not *my* Trip Hetherton. When Claire was visiting us, that's who Trip was calling. I was glad it wasn't me!"

"Too bad. At least Trip doesn't have a room-temperature IQ."

"I like Esteban, Daddy. I'd like to see him again."

"So would I!" my father shot back. "So would I like to see him again!"

"I'll just stroll about and look this place over," Larkin said. "Did your father design it?"

"Yes. All by himself."

What was Dad planning to do about lunch? He was so rattled, he hadn't made his famous spaghetti sauce, and I didn't see any being defrosted.

Larkin had this great scent about her. A perfume so subtle, you only smelled it as she moved around the room, and then very faintly. It was like the smoky smell of burning leaves.

"You know what impresses me most of all?" Larkin asked.

"The table?" My father had paid a fortune for that table.

"The ceiling. It's a very emotional ceiling, very original."

"The ceiling impresses you?"

"With its splash of nails up there in the corner. It's very arresting," Larkin said.

I wanted to tell her that what she thought was emotional was actually a mistake, that what she thought was original and arresting was the "emergency" my father was off taking care of. But I also wanted to watch my father's face when she told him how and why it impressed her.

"It's really very daring," she said. She was looking up at it as if it was the ceiling in the

Sistine Chapel, which my mom and I had seen in Rome the summer before she died. The famous artist Michelangelo had painted it.

"May I tell you something?" I said. I had to tell her.

"Of course, Annabel."

"That is the only thing Dad didn't design. That is a mistake. Esteban calls it 'his bad.'"

"Some mistake. I hope your father keeps it that way."

"I don't think he will. He's furious. My boyfriend bought the wrong size nails while he was working on it."

"Esteban did that?"

"Esteban Santiago. Yes."

"Tell your boyfriend that I like his mistake."

"I wish you would tell Dad that, but don't say Esteban is my boyfriend."

"You told me that already. I remember. Esteban is a Latino, hmm?"

"Yes, a Colombian."

"I will tell Kenny I like it, without mentioning Esteban."

"Thanks, Larkin." Then I thought about lunch again, what Dad would serve her, "Do you like paella?" I asked.

"I love it!"

"Because my father might not have time to make his famous spaghetti sauce. He cooks it for hours."

"Paella takes a long time to prepare, too," she said.

"We have some from the Pantigo Deli."

"That is one of the best delicatessens out here."

"Esteban's uncle works there. Sometimes he cooks there himself."

"You say his name a lot," she said. "He must be special to you."

Another "new" idea of Dad's he got from guess who. I must have blushed. My face felt hot.

Larkin hurried to add, "It's a lovely name. Esteban Santiago."

We talked for a while about what college I wanted to go to when I was graduated in another year. When Mom was dying, a social worker named Elaine had helped our family and become my role model. I wanted a profession where I'd help people. Dad had set an example for Kenyon and me. He volunteered for everything. When a fatherless boy from Seaview came back from Iraq blind and missing a leg, Dad worked on college applications with him, helped him figure out what benefits the Army offered, and walked with him while he learned to use his prosthesis. If you called an ambulance in Seaview, Dad could be giving you oxygen on your way to the hospital. If you were old and alone, he could be the one from Meals on Wheels dropping off soup and a sandwich. Mom said it was sexy the way he cared for others. Did you ever see his face, she'd say, when he talks to those people? Those soft blue eyes?

I'd decided to get a master's in social work. Elaine had said a B.A. was not enough for the good jobs. Think about becoming a therapist, Elaine had said. I told Larkin that was what I wanted to be.

"How will your Esteban fit into this college

picture?" Larkin asked me.

I was glad I didn't have to answer that. I didn't have an answer. Saved by Dad. A second after she said that, he banged through the door shouting, "Is he here? Have you heard from him?"

"No hello for me, Kenny?" Larkin said.

"I'm sorry. Of course I have a hello for you." He went across and held her and kissed her. Then he sighed and said, "That's some ceiling, huh?"

"It is like you, smooth and sweet but with a small nail salad on the side." Larkin chuckled. "That's what I like about you, Kenny. Although you're not an artist yourself, not necessarily a creative person, you don't stand in the way of originality, do you?"

My father was pondering the question, standing there in his work clothes, wearing his old cap, a little grubby, needing a shave. He was looking from the ceiling to Larkin's face. He was trying to figure it out. Was she serious?

"Whether or not you like it," he finally said, "this kid didn't follow my orders."

"He made a mistake," I said.

"I can't afford to have workers make mistakes. And now he's taken off. He makes a mistake and *pfffft*, he beats it."

"Wasn't he home?" I asked.

"They don't have homes, Annabel. They have houses, four and five to a room. They even sleep on the kitchen floor! And no, he was not there. Even Ramón doesn't know where he is, and Ramón always knows where they all are."

"Calm down, honey," said Larkin. "Let me make you a cool drink."

"They don't answer for their mistakes! They run!"

"Who are *they* supposed to be, Dad?"

"The *muchachos*. Hispanics. Latinos. Whatever you call them . . . and they'd better stay away from my daughter!"

"You always say what good workers they are, Kenny."

"Have you ever heard me say I want one of my workers coming to dinner? Have you ever heard me say I want one of them trying to make out with my daughter?"

"He was not trying to make out with me!" I would never think of Esteban in that smarmy way, as though he was doing something to me I didn't want him to do.

"Kenny, please relax and let me make you something cool to drink," said Larkin.

"I need to shower," Dad said.

Next, the sound of Esteban's old Pontiac rattling up our driveway.

"He didn't run!" I said. "He's here!" I left the two of them in the screening room while I rushed out to meet him.

Be still my heart, I thought. It was what Mom used to say when something thrilled her.

EIGHT

"ANNA, I AM SORRY. I came to give you something and to see your father."

"I'm so glad you're here!"

"I never should have left the way I did."

He had on carpenter jeans and an old blue plaid seersucker shirt. The sleeves were so short, his muscles showed.

There were tears behind his eyes and he shook his head. "Oh, Anna, I make apologies for how I talked to you last. I took out on you my great anger with myself for what I had done. I

feel you never see me in a good way. You never
see me smart or going places, becoming someone you can respect. I am less than boys you are
used to, and—"

I put my hand to his lips to hush him. "You
are more to me, not less. Don't ever think that
way, Esteban. I think only good about you. Don't
you know how I feel about you?"

"But I want you to be proud of me and I don't
see how that can happen. Here in this country I
will always be a number zero. Your brother has
college and now will be this animal doctor."

"Shhhh. Listen to yourself. Where is any
mention of how brave you are to be in a foreign
country, working to keep your family together?
Where is any talk about how you sing and so
many flock to Jungle Pete's just to see you?"

"I sing for nothing," he said. "Now I feel your
father is watching me from somewhere inside
with angry eyes. I know he was at Ridge Road
looking for me."

"Is that where you live?"

"If you call it living. *Sí*. I went out the back

61

door as he came in the front. Then I decided to just face him. First I went to town immediately to buy you something because I was bad to leave. You had made everything on the table look like a film."

"Don't be afraid of him, Esteban. He won't bite."

"Just bark."

"Yes, he barks. That he does. But he's not a mean man, Esteban, any more than you're a zero. You are both men I care about. Somehow, some way you have to know each other. When you do, you'll like things about each other. You both love family. You both work hard. Neither of you wishes anyone harm."

We walked very slowly toward the house.

He handed me the package he had, and we stopped while I took a CD out of it.

On the white cover was a line drawing of a large, older woman with black hair. You only saw her from the back.

The title was *Corazón Libre.*

"Free Heart," Esteban said. "It is Mercedes

Sosa. She is who made famous the song you liked."

"Which one?"

"'*Los Niños de Nuestro Olvido*'—'The Children of our Forgetfulness.' She writes folk music about the hard life in Argentina. She is the favorite of my mother, who was born in Buenos Aires."

My father's voice boomed in the muggy carly-afternoon air.

"*Annabel!*"

"I'm coming!"

"He is *muy* angry. I know that from his voice."

"Thank you for this present, Esteban."

"It is because you liked the song and because I never shared the paella dinner with you. My bad."

"You made a mistake, that's all."

"Another mistake. . . . Will he not want me to see you now?"

"Esteban?"

"What, Anna?"

I took his hand. "Don't think so much about my father now. Esteban, it is not going to be easy for us. But we will have to find a way to make things work."

He squeezed my hand hard. "We will have to," he said. "I am okay with that."

"And I am okay with that too."

"Thank you for thinking we can, Anna."

NINE

THESE WERE the rules.

1. I was not to have Esteban to our house.
2. I was not to watch him play soccer.
3. I was not to go to Jungle Pete's on Saturday nights.
4. I was not to go to the Pantigo Deli.
5. I was not to telephone him or receive calls from him, and Dad took away my cell phone.

He kept the screening room ceiling as it was, and he even paid Esteban the usual ten dollars an hour.

"I am a fair businessman," Dad told me, "but I am a loving parent as well. I paid this *mucha-cho* as I said I would, despite his incompetence. But he had better stay away from you, Annabel. What is the matter with you, running out the door to greet him?"

"I like him, that's all."

"You're right, that's all."

I almost never did what Dad said I couldn't do, but he had not forbidden me to walk along the ocean with Esteban, and that's what we were doing. Okay, that's a tacky way to put it. I was defying Dad on a major issue. My excuse to myself was that I wouldn't do it for long. Somehow I'd find a way for Dad to accept Esteban. My father was not a petty man. He was a kind, caring, gruff guy with a big heart, and there'd be a way to reach him. I'd find it.

Esteban said where he came from there were beautiful coral reefs and the sea was a turquoise color, but the beaches were small and narrow.

We walked along, arms around each other. With him, even that didn't seem that innocent. I could feel warm little darts running from inside my elbows to the tips of my fingers.

"Is there anything I can do to change your father's mind about me seeing you?" Esteban asked.

"Not right now. Maybe he'll change his mind later on."

"Is it most because I am not from this country?"

"That is a lot of it, yes. He feels about you the way Gioconda feels about me. You seem to him to be a threat to our family. We are very close, too, particularly since Mom died."

It was after five, a foggy afternoon, with the tide coming in, both of us barefoot, pants rolled up, shoes back on Main Beach.

"I hear he treats his men well and he is not a bad man to work for."

"He is not a bad man, Esteban."

"You're right. He is just afraid, like my sister. Does your brother feel as he does?"

"Kenyon doesn't judge people that way."

"He is not prejudiced?"

"No. My father isn't really prejudiced, either. He's just a little behind the times."

"Except when it comes to knowing who will work for nuts."

"*Peanuts.* We don't say someone works for nuts. We say someone works for peanuts."

"That's us," Esteban said gloomily.

"Do you wish you weren't here?" I asked him.

"Well, Anna, I am a Colombian. Providencia is my home."

"So why are you here?"

"You don't want me to be here?"

"I want you here, oh yes! But sometimes I wonder why you came all this way." I knew that I sounded impatient with him when what I really felt was frustrated that we had to sneak around to be together.

"Our family cannot exist there on what little they have. Gioconda and I help support our younger brothers and sisters in Providencia. Two boys, three girls, and my mother's parents live with us. We are all ten family. *El orgullo del*

Hispano está en la familia. Do you know what that says in English?"

"Tell me."

"A Hispanic's pride is in his family."

"Do you know what Esteban is in English? Stephen. I may call you Stephen sometimes."

"Ay, no! Don't anglicize my name. Never!"

"Oh?" I was surprised he was so adamant.

He said, "Ramón got so mad when a *vato* in our house had a boss who changed his name from Rafael to Ralph. Ramón teaches we must keep our names and our pride!"

"And what is this Ramón all about, anyway?"

"Ramón is *familia* here, in our house *her*e. We are loyal to each other, which is why I can never be a Stephen."

I had to laugh. He was so solemn at times. I bumped against him purposely and said, "You are such a wack!"

"Because I listen to Ramón? He knows the rope. He has all the answers."

"Ropes," I said.

"What?"

I knew he didn't like it when I corrected his English.

"Nothing," I said. "It is nothing."

"See if you can catch me," he said. He ran ahead of me, splashing in the waves while I ran after him. It was not easy to catch him. I know he slowed up on purpose so that I could.

Where we were on the beach, there was no one. Even if others had been there, we would hardly have seen them, the fog was so thick.

That was what I loved about Seaview beaches. There were private parts, and when we found one, we would go up to the dunes and talk and make out.

There was always that moment when Esteban would stop touching me. At the same time he would hold my hands so I couldn't touch him.

"We don't need a chaperone with you doing that all the time," I complained.

"One of us has to."

"Why?"

He smiled at me. "The Swan Man has to keep us out of trouble."

"I like that you remember my nickname for you. But I don't like you to be the one who says what we can do and not do."

"I think sometimes you would not say anything to stop us. Did you stop Trip, too?"

"I never had to. I didn't want him." That much was true. I'd wanted to be with him and be seen with him, but I'd never felt the physical pull with Trip that I felt with Esteban.

"Do you swear that's true?" Esteban asked me.

"I swear! But why do you ask me so much about Trip?"

He smoothed my hair back from my face. He had such small hands.

I remembered a poem by e. e. cummings with the line "nobody, not even the rain, has such small hands."

He said, "Maybe why is because I might be falling in love with you."

"Maybe? Might be?"

"I wait to see," he said. "Do you understand?"

"I wait to see too," I said, "but I think I know now. I think we both know."

Our mouths opened to each other, our arms held us tight.

What a time for me to see Larkin over Esteban's shoulder, Larkin walking her dog, one of those golden hound dogs all the guys in trucks have riding in the back!

Can they ever just go on with their walks? Do they always have to run up for a smell, panting, wagging their tails, and shaking water all over us?

"Oh, no, it's Larkin and Dolly!" I said, pushing Esteban away.

"So it takes Larkin to make you stop us?"

She was coming toward us, barefoot in cutoff white jeans and a navy tank top.

"Come on, Dolly! Come!"

Dolly was licking Esteban's face and neck. The first time I'd met Dolly, she'd tried to hump my leg.

"Why did she have to come along?" I muttered.

Then Larkin saw us. "Hello!"

"Hi, Larkin." She was walking toward us, carrying Dolly's leash.

"You remember Esteban," I said. It had been a while since the matinee incident. My brother was almost graduated from college. In three days I would go to Cornell with Dad for the ceremony.

"Hello, Esteban." She smiled.

"Hello, Missus. You know, I never thanked you for saying you liked my mistake."

"I do like it, and you're welcome. Come, Dolly!"

I was glad she didn't stop to talk, and not sure if she was embarrassed or just wanted to let us have our privacy. She knew that Esteban and I were forbidden to see each other. Right in front of me one day my father said to her, "If you ever see the famous Latino roof designer around here, call me immediately so I can bring home one of those pest bombs. After I smoke him out, I'll report him to the law for living ten people to

73

a room. He's not exactly the kind I want anywhere near my daughter."

Larkin had no answer to that. She'd learned to let my father rant and rave. It'd be over faster that way. The more noise he made, the less it mattered. When he was quiet, he was lethal.

This time the dog followed her, and I watched them until they disappeared into the fog.

"That was bad timing," Esteban said.

"I'll say."

"Will she tell your father she saw us together?"

"I think she'll tell him and make him swear not to tell me she did."

"I bet she won't tell him," Esteban said. "She's too nice."

"But she's crazy about my father."

"Let's make a bet," he said. "What do you want to bet?"

"If she tells him, you can never grab my hands and stop me from touching you."

He frowned and shook his head, playing with the gold Santa Cecilia medal around his neck.

"It was your idea to bet," I reminded him. "Don't welsh."

"What is that? The rabbit made with cheese? Once where I cooked that was on the menu."

"Not Welsh rarebit. *Welsh!* It means you don't keep a promise."

"All right," he sighed. "But if the Missus *doesn't* tell your father, I will always be our chaperone. You will never complain about it, or pout."

"I can still pout."

He said, "But I will be the boss of such things. . . . How will we know if she is a squeaker?"

"Squealer." Sometimes I *had* to correct him. "Oh, we'll know. Don't worry about that! If you think it's hard to see each other now, wait until he hears about it!" Then I said, "What do you have against sex?"

If he was blushing I couldn't tell, but he had an embarrassed expression on his face. He looked away from me as he said, "It is too soon for us to take that step, Anna."

"Is that for you to say or me?" I asked him.

"It is for us both to say. We just don't want it to be an accident."

"The last accident you had is now a piece of art."

"But if *we* have one, I don't think your father will look at it that way."

I said, "It's none of his business. You don't get it, do you? I'm not a child, Esteban! Next thing I know, you'll proof me."

He pulled me down beside him. "That's not the next thing." He smiled. "This is."

That was when I got the idea to steal one of Kenyon's condoms. I knew there were still some Trojans under his shorts in my bottom drawer. What if I had one with me at a time like this?

TEN

OWNSTAIRS IN THE Seaview Library was a
book called *La Paella de Valencia*. It was
on a bottom shelf alongside other cook-
books, and I could see that the last time it
had been borrowed was in 2000. That became
our mailbox. We left notes saying where we
would be, and sometimes we just left love notes.
It was easy for me, because in the summer I
worked there five days a week. Esteban was at
the deli most of the time or on another job, but
he didn't have a problem running in there late

afternoons during free moments. Besides, he liked to read books from the Spanish collection, which had grown so large in the last few years that it occupied several shelves on the main floor.

Esteban's favorite writer was a fellow Colombian: Gabriel García Márquez. He said everyone at home loved him, and they all called him Gabo.

I left Esteban bits of poetry I liked, particularly my new favorite, e. e. cummings.

One of his poems began, "i like my body when it is with your body."

Esteban wrote back, "Did you know my lucky initial is E for my mother's first name? Now you do, Anna, my love, and when I am not your Swan Man, I will be e. e. santiago."

Once my message to him was: "My father sees a client on Sunday morning. Will you be on Main Beach? Nine to eleven? Xxxxxx."

He answered, "Sweet Woman, Sunday mornings are hard for me to get away. Gioconda and I go to Casa Pentecostal with our housemates, and then we all sit down for Sunday dinner. I am working that afternoon helping a man in Watermill put in a lawn. What other time can we meet next week? ees"

We'd brought Kenyon home from college the last week in June, so it was just as well that Esteban was busy, because my brother would need help packing for the move to his apartment.

People say we look enough alike to be twins, both of us blond and blue-eyed, both of us on the skinny side and tall.

The one thing I really liked about my brother was that he never tried to talk me into or out of anything. We didn't agree on every subject, but he didn't pull rank on me.

He asked me how I'd like to bike down to Accabonac Presbyterian with him. That way we'd exercise our minds, bodies, and souls.

"We can get coffee and a bagel first," he said. "Does the Accabonac General Store still have benches outside?"

"I thought you'd like help packing."

He said, "There's plenty of time to do that. I

need a good sermon. Reverend Stewart is still in the pulpit, isn't he?"

"Yes." I'd almost forgotten that side of Kenyon. When Mom was alive, he always went to church with her. Dad and I made excuses at times, but Kenyon never did. Once Mom died, I never went to church except with Dad on Christmas.

"Don't tell me you still feel the same way about church, Anna B.?" He sounded sad. Mom used to call me Anna B.

"Why would I feel any differently?"

"I thought you might have changed. You don't seem to be upset because Dad is dating Larkin."

"Larkin didn't let Mom die."

"God didn't either, Sis."

"He didn't do anything to stop it!"

"God didn't give Mama breast cancer, Annabel."

When Kenyon was feeling sad about her death, he always called her Mama.

"I thought the Lord gaveth and tooketh," I

said. "If He didn't giveth, He didn't taketh either, did He? He let her suffer. Remember how long it went on?"

"Let's change the subject. Why don't you take a walk on the beach with your new boyfriend? Now's your chance, isn't it? Dad will be going to the Unitarian church with Larkin."

I knew I was safe telling Kenyon all about Esteban. Since both Esteban and I were in one piece, Dad couldn't have known we were seeing each other secretly.

"I'll bike with you to the Accabonac store and have a bagel and coffee with you," I said.

I couldn't admit that my new boyfriend was going to church himself.

"You don't have to," Kenyon said. "Aren't we going to have Sunday dinner as usual?"

"With Larkin, too," I said. "You must have guessed that."

"I like her, Annabel. I think she's good for Dad."

"Because he's going to church suddenly?"

"Well, he never went with Mom."

"He was too tired. It's his only day off,

remember. He didn't go because he didn't need to go," I said. "He had everything he wanted. Now he goes because he wants Larkin."

"He's really hooked on her, too," Kenyon said. "You know what's in the screening room?"

"The new three-legged end table she made?" She called it High Heels. It really had legs, too, wearing high heels.

"The high-heeled table plus a smelly, wet, gold dog," said Kenyon.

"Larkin must have taken her swimming."

"Dogs like that don't need to go anywhere to smell," said Kenyon. "And that dog is a male."

"A male named Dolly?"

"D-a-l-i," Kenyon said. "Salvador Dalí. The artist with the long mustache who painted those strange clocks and watches."

"I never heard of him."

"He was quite a character."

"Like Larkin," I said.

"But I like her, Annabel. She's really cool."

I liked her too—a lot. It was good to see Dad smiling again, and I didn't really think I'd win the bet with Esteban. She wasn't a squealer, or I would have heard from Dad by now. So Esteban was still calling the shots, and I was still a seventeen-year-old virgin.

ELEVEN

Every Fourth of July celebration my father went to Mom's brother's on the North Shore, to help with the kids and the fireworks. He wanted to miss our own big celebration down on Main Beach, because Mom and he had always gone to it. That would be okay with me this year, because I could go with Esteban.

Most years, great crowds gathered at Main by the time it was dark, and the sky lit up with rockets, roman candles, fire snakes, sparkling fountains, spinners, sparklers, any kind of fireworks you could imagine. People wore green glow-in-the-dark cuffs and glow headbands so we didn't bump into each other walking along on the sand, and everyone from little kids to old grandmas and grandpas turned out for the celebration.

The town put on the show for us, but that year the Saturday-night fireworks were canceled because of the piping plovers. The North Shore did not have the problem.

"What are piping plovers?" Esteban asked me.

"They're little birds. You can hardly see them, they're so small. But they're an endangered species. This year they've nested right in the dunes. Their tiny eggs are hatching, and the fireworks would interfere."

Kenyon was with us as we walked along the bay down at Barnes Landing late that afternoon. He said he wanted to meet Esteban. Someone in the family had to see what this man was all about.

"You cancel your freedom celebration for

baby birds?" Esteban asked us.

"These little guys come all the way from Patagonia every year," said Kenyon. "They fly roughly sixty-four hundred miles, unprotected, uncharted, trying to avoid the pitfalls nature sets for them. Bad weather, hawks, eagles, even killer doves."

"And us," I said.

"And man," Kenyon agreed. "So this year the town decided not to interfere with their babies being born. We canceled the noise *and* the people."

Everyone in Seaview was talking about it. Most people were willing to make that sacrifice for the birds. But there was one newspaper owner who was so against it that he printed a recipe for Baked Piping Plover.

I was a little downhearted, because I wanted to show Esteban what a Fourth of July celebration was like.

Esteban said, "We have our own *día de la independencia*. Ours is on the twentieth of July. But we have celebrations every chance we get:

festivals, fairs, fiestas, carnivals, pageants. Almost every day there is a celebration going on somewhere in our country. In the states you only hear about our trouble."

"Would you stop one of those celebrations for piping plovers, do you think?" Kenyon asked.

"We have a crab migration in May to June. Even roads close for it."

"Then it sounds like you would," Kenyon said.

"My brother's going to be a veterinarian. He loves all critters," I explained to Esteban.

"I knew he was to be a doctor," Esteban said. I knew what Esteban was thinking, that there was no way he could ever be anything like a doctor, that to himself he was a "number zero."

Kenyon said, "I care about saving endangered species."

"I, too, feel that way." Esteban smiled. "And I don't even have a vote."

"None of us do in this matter," I said.

"Who will you work for, Kenyon?" Esteban asked.

"Dr. Annan. Do you know him?"

"I know of him."

"What do *you* plan to be, Esteban?" Kenyon asked.

"Maybe I will learn a business here, and be a carpenter or something someday back in Providencia."

"You have no plans to stay here?" Kenyon asked.

"I could not afford here. I'm part of a big family," Esteban said. "It is hard enough now to find any place I am not sharing with many others. And except for my sister, they are not family."

I didn't like the conversation. I wondered if it was Kenyon's subtle way of showing me Esteban had no plans to stay here permanently. Part of me probably knew that already, but not a part I was letting myself believe.

Next thing I knew, Esteban had reached for my hand, maybe sensing what I was feeling, maybe feeling it himself.

He changed the subject. "Where I live," he said, "we have this place called Morgan's Island.

"Henry Morgan, the pirate," Kenyon said.
"We have a rum named after him."

Esteban was playfully bumping into me, and
I would try to trip him with my foot. I think
Kenyon got the message. He glanced at his
watch and said something about being late for
an appointment.

He went back the other way after he told
Esteban he hoped to see him again.

"He is a good fellow," Esteban said.

"He gets me through everything."

"What do you have to get through?"

"My mom's death." I didn't mention that last
summer at this time I had been dumped by Trip,
finally, too. How had Trip put it? He thought we
should "take a breather" from each other.

Esteban said, "If I ever lost *mi madre*, I would
have great difficulty getting through it, as you
say. You are lucky to be close with your brother.
Sometimes Gioconda tries to help me with
things, but she behaves too much like a boss."

"She's mean-mouthed, too. Kenyon isn't."

"Does he like to work for that Dr. Annan?"

"Seaview Veterinarian is the best there is."

"I didn't mean the hospital," Esteban said. "I meant the doctor."

"What's the matter with Dr. Annan?"

"Nothing, I guess," Esteban said. "There is an Annan on our street who causes us trouble. Maybe I have the wrong man."

"You must have. Everybody in Seaview likes Charlie Annan, Esteban."

"I could make a mistake then. I mix names up."

"But he's the only Dr. Annan out here."

"You know, Annabel, I think you confuse my brain. Is that what you want to do to me? Corrupt my brain so I don't know anything anymore?" He put his arms around my waist, grinning at me. "Tell me you will not do that to me."

"Where can we go now?" I said. "It looks like rain. We only have three hours until you go to work. I don't dare take you home. We could dance under the awning at Main Beach."

90

"I know what I want to do," he said. "Go to cinema."

"A movie? On a holiday weekend? We'd never get in."

"This is a Spanish film. But there are English subtitles."

Esteban was talking about the Saturday-night Latino cinema at the recreation center.

"This will be a great favor to me," he said. "I miss films. My sister tunes in only what *she* wants on our television."

"If you really want to go to the movies, sure. We'll go."

On the walk over to the rec center Esteban said, "I have said what I will maybe become someday and your brother will work for the veterinarian. What will you do, Anna?"

"I want to be a social worker. Maybe work with Latinos. Dad says *he* wants to take Spanish as a second language. I already pick up copies of *The Bilingual News* that they drop off in the library."

"*El Bilingue*? I read the *horoscopo* in that. We

are both *Sagitarios, sí?*"

"That means we are both adventurous, Swan Man."

He was silent for a while, and then he said, "Will you have to go to college to be a social worker?"

"Yes. I haven't decided if I'll go to Boston or to Chicago. And it's not all up to me. I have to be accepted."

"Of course," said Esteban. "When will you go?"

"The year after next."

"I am glad that you go," he said, "but I am not glad too."

We didn't say much the rest of the way. I sensed he felt the same way I did, that suddenly we saw the future and we weren't together.

TWELVE

THE MOVIE WAS called *Maria Full of Grace*. It starred this Colombian named Catalina Sandino Moreno. She was a real hottie. It was about a pregnant teenager who became a drug mule to make money for her family.

Esteban let me hold his hand, and when I say "let me," that's what I mean, because he was far more interested in what we were watching than he was in us.

On the way out, we stopped to talk to three boys Esteban introduced as friends. They called him Teban. Esteban said they were his friends from home.

"Home in Seaview? Or home in Colombia?" I asked."

"Both," said Esteban. "Except Ramón. He is from Peru."

."I'm Dario," the tallest fellow said. "You have *me* to thank for meeting my *compañero*. I couldn't work that day."

"Yes. Dario. Pleased to meet you."

"I hope you are not *el tornado* like the boss," Dario said.

Chino, the short one, rolled his eyes to the sky, which was beginning to become storm dark.

I said, "Did my father bawl you out for letting Esteban work for you?"

Two of the boys bent double laughing, but Ramón did not even smile. His expression was very serious, and he seemed to be judging me, looking me all over but not in a sexy way.

Dario said, "*Muy enojado!* Angry!"

"Esteban, you didn't tell me my dad bawled out Dario."

"He bawl everyone out," Chino told me.

I said, "I just see him get very quiet when he's angry, like he's smoldering."

Dario held his hand up, suppressing a grin. "Listen! *Señor* Brown is a good man. He's not like some who don't care about their workers. He gave me money ahead of my paycheck once when I needed to get a bill collector off my back. Good boss!"

Finally Ramón almost smiled while he nodded in agreement. He said something in Spanish and they all laughed.

Then Esteban began talking about the actress Catalina Sandino Moreno. I'd always wished I wasn't a blonde, that I was a brunette like her, and I wouldn't mind having a name like that, instead of Annabel Brown.

"You know what?" Esteban said. "She was nominated for the American Academy Award for that film."

"And she is from Colombia!" Chino said.

"The first time anyone was ever nominated for Best Actress who spoke entirely in Spanish," Esteban said.

Dario said, "But she can speak English. I read that."

"So that's how your country looks?" I said.

"Not our country. Ecuador," Chino said.

"It was filmed in Ecuador, not Colombia, but we have the drugs, the mules. That is accurate." Esteban put his arm around me. "Most Colombian girls do not deal drugs, though. They live with their families until they're twenty-five, then get jobs and get married."

"Who Teban likes is Shakira," said Dario.

"Who doesn't like her?" Esteban said.

"She is a Colombian, too," Chino said. "She was in a *telenovela, El Oasis. Ai*, beautiful beautiful."

Esteban told me, "Our *telenovelas* are like your soap operas."

Chino poked him and said, "You get off the subject of Shakira, *ese*."

96

Esteban continued, "Except our *telenovelas* have an end, and your soap serials never end."

Chino said, "If Shakira was on the TV here, I would wish it to never never end."

"You too, Esteban?" I asked.

"I preferred Thalia if I watched any *tele-novela*," said Esteban.

Ramón was not a talker, at least not there, not that night, but he did put in: "Here you like American better, Teban, or it seems so when you get the remote. You act like a coconut."

"Old American films," said Chino. *"Muchas gringas."*

"SIDA," Ramón said.

"Callarse!" Esteban told him.

There was a little mock punching back and forth, and Chino said something else in Spanish that made Esteban really punch him. Where had my two years of Spanish gone?

They bantered a few minutes more while I watched everyone come out of the recreation center. I didn't recognize a soul.

* * *

Before he went on to Jungle Pete's, Esteban drove me to my corner just as it was starting to rain. He kissed me for a long, slow time, and I could see his solemn brown eyes, which were always open and looking at me when I opened mine. Sometimes I'd tell myself, *Memorize this moment, Anna B.,* as though some part of me knew it was too good, too full. How could it last?

"Why do they call you Teban and *ese*?" I said.

"Teban is short for Esteban. We call each other *ese*. It is a nickname such as this afternoon you call me Wack."

"No, honey, I said you *were* a wack. I didn't call you Wack. What did Ramón mean, you act like a coconut?"

"Coconut means brown outside and white inside. The homies tease about white girls."

"Because of me. White isn't good to your friends, is it?"

"As good as brown is to yours, Anna. All these questions."

"I'm sorry. I like Chino. He's very friendly."

"We all like him. His only family, an older brother, was dragged off by the enemy and Chino never saw him again. That's why he came here, to forget and make money."

"Colombia sounds so dangerous, E.E."

"Yes. It is not safe for many. But let's talk of us, and when we meet next." He leaned over and kissed me on the lips. "Sunday is never good," he said. "It is when we homies all have the big meal after I come from Casa Pentecostal. Evenings we study with Ramón."

"Study what?"

"We do spiritual study. Ramón is a deep, deep man."

"I thought you were a Catholic?"

"When I go home I will be one again. The *familia* is Catholic. But here I like this church better. I go there with Ramón and Virgil."

"What does—I hope I pronounce this right—what does *regresaremos pronto* mean? I see it on the sermon board out front of Casa Pentecostal."

"It means we will be home soon. In heaven. With God," said Esteban. "When can we meet on

99

Monday? My eyes will be sore from not seeing you, Anna."

"I'll leave a note in the paella book, E.E."

"Monday I have no work after six o'clock."

"Maybe we'll have a moonlight picnic, if we have a moon."

"Wait! I have something for you, Anna."

He handed me a box from Victoria's Secret, a new store on Main Street. It said "Anna Sui— *Secret Wish*." It was a shower gel with a card saying, "Secret Wish is a fragrance of magical power. Close your eyes and wish. Anything is possible once you release this enchanting essence of a fairy tale."

I took off the top and put a little on my wrist, then on his.

"I love the aroma!"

He smelled it and grinned. "I hope that's not us. I hope we're not a fairy tale. That's *my* wish."

"It's mine too, E.E."

He turned the key and the motor started. "Take my jacket to cover your head," he said. He gave me a two-fingered salute. "Don't get

100

too wet, sweet girl."

We wouldn't have dared a drive to the house. Dad could be back from the North Shore by then.

Later, I told Kenyon, "I met some of Esteban's buddies tonight. I've never seen him around any other Latinos except the soccer players. It was interesting to hear him talk about movies and singers he loved from his country. I think sometimes he's homesick."

"I could tell that in the little time we spent together today. He loved talking about Providencia and his family."

"And while he's a Catholic at home, here he goes to Casa Pentecostal."

"That sermon board out front of that church makes a lot of locals mad, Dr. Annan claims," said Kenyon.

"Why would it make anyone mad? It just says they're all going to heaven."

"Charlie says it means they'll all go back to their homes soon, where they send all their money. They will never think of themselves as Americans."

"That's not what Esteban told me. He said it means going home to God."

"There's no mention of God, though."

"Esteban wouldn't lie to me."

Kenyon said, "When you first fall in love, it's hard to see the person. You're too excited."

"Last year I thought I was in love with Trip Hetherton, but I wasn't so excited that I couldn't see he was boring. I just loved his looks—and the things his money bought: the Boxster, the sailboat. But I can't remember him ever buying me anything except tickets to movies or dances. He never bought me a gift."

"Who was it who said there's no there there? I think it was Gertrude Stein describing Trip," Kenyon said.

"For the first time tonight I really saw Esteban. He wanted badly to go to that movie. He watched it so intensely. Trip would have chosen *Star Wars* or something with Angelina Jolie in it."

"Well, Trip isn't from Colombia."

"And for the first time Esteban and I talked about my plan to be a social worker. We didn't talk about it very long. I think it depressed both of us, thinking about the future."

Kenyon was finishing packing his things to take to his new apartment. He was such a long drink of water compared to Esteban, using his long arms to sling shirts across to his suitcase on the bed. My bottom bureau drawer was almost empty.

He said, "Sis? Do me a favor. Don't sleep with that guy for a long, long time. He's not the kind of fellow who's going to appreciate easy."

And that very second there went the condoms in one of his big hands, from the bureau to his bag.

Kenyon added, "You're just starting to get to know him, Anna B. What's the big rush?"

"No one's rushing," I said, "but since when did *you* appoint yourself pope?"

"All I mean is their women usually hold out for marriage—at least the ones they respect and marry do."

"So I'd be a slut if I was easy?"

"Even if easy wasn't part of the equation."

Did I need that crack of lightning over the roof for emphasis?

"And where are your girlfriends this summer? Where's Mitzi?" Kenyon asked.

"We're not kids anymore, Kenyon. We have jobs, boyfriends, lives."

"Don't be in too big a hurry to grow up," he said.

THIRTEEN

Mitzi Graney stopped in at the library to check out *Tender Is the Night*. Seniors at Seaview High had F. Scott Fitzgerald on their summer reading list—any book of his. I'd chosen *The Crackup*, which was almost like a journal, a dark and depressing one, I thought. Kenyon said I was just too untouched by life so far to appreciate it.

"I already read some of *Tender*," Mitzi said. "It's so old-fashioned. This character has his shorts in a twist over whether or not some babe's a virgin. Speaking of which, you could have lost your V and be pregnant, for all I really know about you anymore. Claire said when she visited you, she got stuck with Trip because you were never around."

"Claire always had the hots for Trip anyway."

"But where've you been? Your cell phone isn't even connected. I still haven't got my Mac fixed or I'd have e-mailed you. What's going on?"

"I'm helping my brother get settled at Dr. Annan's."

"That's not what I hear. Virgil says you're seeing Esteban Santiago."

"I was going to tell you. Dad's so against it. He took my cell phone away. I didn't want word to get around town before I tell Dad myself."

"Oh, that'll be a pretty scene. Did this start the night we went to Jungle Pete's?"

"I saw Esteban before that, playing soccer in the fields behind the school. Now I see him whenever we can manage it. I've been telling Dad I'm with *you* Monday nights. It's Dad's poker night, so it's not likely he'd want to reach me. Do you mind that I did that?"

"Of course not. But be careful, Annabel."

"Careful about what?"

"Dating one of them from Ridge Road isn't as easy as you think."

"You sound just like my dad, saying 'one of them.'"

Mitzi said, "They're different, Annabel. At least the ones in *that* house are. By the time you learn that, it's too late."

"What do you mean?"

"Have you heard about Ramón? He got Esteban and Virgil to leave Holy Family for the Casa."

"Esteban said Ramón is spiritual, deep."

"Deep!" Mitzi spat out. "He's not deep. He's trouble! Call me when we can really talk. Can we make a date now?"

"I was just going to ask her that myself," Esteban's voice said suddenly, and there he stood at the checkout desk, grinning at us.

He said, "Someone took our paella book, Anna."

It was a sunny July Monday, so it was quiet in the library. A lot of people were at the beach or on the tennis courts and golf courses. Monday nights Esteban and I saw each other for sure. Other times we fit each other in, depending on where Dad went and what jobs Esteban was on. Whenever he could, Esteban came to the beach where I took my lunch every day.

Even though Mitzi had met him when we were at Jungle Pete's, I introduced her to him, glad that for once he was taller than the girl. Mitzi was five-foot-two, dark Irish, with green eyes. At Seaview High we were part of the Vestal Virgins, a group that was getting smaller and smaller every year. We'd named ourselves that in fun. The fast crowd called us The Pesty Virgins.

Esteban put on the charm, laughing down into her eyes, that funny one tooth of his sticking out. "Hello, Señorita Graney."

Mitzi flashed him a smile and touched my arm. "Call me. Please, Annabel? I miss you so!"

"I will. I promise."

"I will see that she does," said Esteban.

"My good friend," I told Esteban as she left.

"Virgil's *gringuita*."

"Is that what you call me, too? A *gringuita*?"

"If that's all right with you."

"I'm never sure if *gringa* is a good thing to be called."

"I'm never sure if Latino is." Esteban chuckled. Then he leaned on the front desk and told me, "*Te quiero*. Can I say that to you in here?" He looked around, then looked back at me with those serious brown eyes.

"Me, too. *Estoy enamorada*."

"Lovely, *mi dulce*. Your Spanish is good!"

"It'll be even better after I start the SSL course in September."

"I'm glad you're going to do that. It is better to make love with you in my language. It is made for love."

I could feel my cheeks get hot and I knew they were red. He could always do that to me. "When will we meet tonight?"

Then he seemed to be stalling, to want to say something he couldn't. I waited him out until he

109

had to speak. "I planned I'd have tonight off, but now it seems I don't." He looked so guilty. Our plans had changed before when we had to cancel things, but I hadn't seen that look on his face. His eyes couldn't meet mine.

"What do you have to do tonight? Dad is going to Larkin's after his poker game. Kenyon has moved out. We would have the place to ourselves."

"I don't take the chance to be at your house, Anna. You know that. I feel I am going to be beat up any minute. Your father will crash through the door and punch me hard."

"Then we'll go someplace else," I told Esteban. There wasn't anyplace else that private, but we often went down to Main Beach at night with his boom box and a blanket.

"Not tonight. I'm sorry. There is a special man coming to La Casa tonight."

"The church? You're going to church instead of keeping our date? You were just in church yesterday!"

Esteban said, "This man coming to our

church is the Latino Billy Graham. You know the name Billy Graham?"

"The preacher."

"Yes. This man is like him but for us. There is little opportunity to hear this man, they say. I would ask you to come too, but I do not think he would have an interpreter."

"Are you going with your sister?"

"She has dinner to get for everyone. I made no plans to go with anyone, Anna. Ramón and Virgil may go. I believe it is a once-in-a-lifetime chance to hear a great Latino preacher."

"I want to come with you, E.E."

"You know, I like to be E. E. Santiago. Estrella is the birth name of *mi madre*. E is lucky for me. She gave me my Santa Cecilia medal."

"Did you hear me say I'd like to go to church with you?"

"I heard you, Anna. I heard you."

"Well?"

"What for, Anna? His message will not be for you."

"It doesn't matter. I'll see what the Casa is like."

111

"Come if you want to so badly," said Esteban.

I didn't believe there was a heaven, but if there was one, my mother would be looking down and grinning. Anything to get me to church—any church.

"I do want to come. I want to know every-thing about you, even if it involves going to church."

"I have the God you don't believe in to thank for getting you to my church," said Esteban, smiling, touching me playfully under the chin.

"What is this preacher's name?"

"Antolin. He goes by one name only."

"Like Larkin."

He frowned and shook his head. "Are you serious about this? Antolin is not in the same sentence with Larkin."

"I'm sorry, Esteban. I shouldn't kid around."

"No, you should not."

"I am really sorry." I was. Why couldn't I just accept the fact that Esteban was religious? I wondered if it threatened me in some way, if it divided us.

Esteban said, "Be careful, *cariña*. Antolin may cast a spell on you. They say he is very, very dynamite."

"Would you like it if I was religious?"

"What is anything without God?" Esteban said.

"I can't believe in a God. I wish I could, but I'm an atheist."

"No one is an atheist, Anna. That means you declare flatly there is no God. You mean to say that you are an agnostic. That means you just don't know."

"I'm with the ones who declare flatly," I said. "Who taught you the difference between the two?"

"I learned most of my English in school, at home. But here I took ESL at the high school on Tuesday nights."

"Why, Esteban?"

"Why did I take more? The better you speak, the easier it becomes to get good jobs. A man who was in our house is now boss of a construction crew. He can be boss of all the ones who work with him because he is able to speak for them. They don't understand what the *gringos* say they want done."

"May I really go with you tonight? Is it okay?"

Esteban sighed, shrugged. "All right! I wanted to give you a *pañuelo*, anyway. Now you will need it to go with me."

"A bandanna like the one you wore when you first came to my house?"

"Yes, I got you one not even knowing you were coming to the Casa. I just wanted you to have one."

"Another present, E. E.?" I'd never given him a gift, because I was afraid he'd feel he had to reciprocate. "Thank you, Esteban, but I hope you're not spending all your money on me."

"Only what little is mine to spend. I send the most to my family, but I like to give things to you. Then you always have something I picked out. Tonight, wear the *pañuelo* like a scarf, a belt. Tie it on your wrist or ankle. Yellow, blue, red: the colors of our Colombian flag. We all wear our colors, but in church we are *una gente*. One people."

114

"Why don't I wear the American flag?"

"Because at the Casa we wear the colors of our homelands, and you are my guest. You will see plenty of red, white, and blue. It will be the three colors you will see the most of, but in *our* flags. Virgil would be a big exception, because he would wear green, white, and red. For Mexico."

Since we weren't busy in the library, I told Miss Chidister I was taking a small break. I knew she was wise to what was going on with Esteban and me. When I'd asked her if she would suggest Spanish classes to the programmer, she said she was sure I could wait until fall when the high school taught SSL evenings. "He's not going anywhere, is he?" she said.

"Who are you talking about?" I tried to play dumb, but she winked at me and shook her head, as though she was in on our secret.

Esteban and I went out the back door and sat on the bench where the employees who still smoked sat. Esteban was in bib overalls, the high kind he didn't wear a shirt under, just his skin and his religious medal. I'd noticed Miss

Chidister giving him a look. We didn't have a dress code in the library. Customers came in shorts all the time. There was just something slightly naked-looking about Esteban and his brown skin, shoulders, arms; you could see his nipples.

"Does Mitzi ever go to the Casa?" I asked him. I'd know the answer to that myself if I'd ever hang out with her again. Free time wasn't anything I knew about since Esteban.

"No, no Mitzi. Virgil and Ramón don't bring guests."

"What made you three leave Holy Family? The music at the Casa? I hear it sometimes when I'm driving to the IGA Sundays."

I knew I was trying to keep him with me, stalling, asking questions, anything.

"I like the music at Casa Pentecostal. I do. Very much. But that is not the reason. At Catholic church it is the same thing over and over. A sermon that has nothing to do with us, then recitations, some even in Latin."

"Still? I thought they stopped that."

"Not in all churches. Has there ever been a Hispanic pope? There are not even many priests here who can speak our language. Even though I speak English, things I say in confession have no discussion. They say how many Hail Marys to recite for penance and tell me to go."

"Is it different in Providencia?"

"Catholic churches are often the same everywhere. But here we are needy in a new way, in a country we don't know. A nun came to our door once where we all live. Chino was very sick, and we thought she had come to help him because we tried to get a nurse nun to visit him. This nun knew nothing about Chino. She had come to collect for the new convent. The one they built overlooking the ocean. You know how much that cost? Millions of dollars, and they go from house to house of poor people who have trouble even paying the rent."

"It isn't fair, I know."

"What is, Anna?" Then he stood up. "I see there is a notice about computer lessons. Find out when they give them, would you please,

Anna? I need to learn what everyone seems to know. I will never get anywhere if I do not become modern."

"If you get a computer, we can e-mail each other."

"Ramón has one I can always use. I just have to learn how. I feel dumb not knowing how. And I am not dumb, Anna!"

"I know you're not. And I'll help you."

"They say never let your girlfriend teach you how to drive, so maybe it is the same with computers. Besides, I do not want you to see I know nothing about the internet. You and your friends know so much. I want to learn, Anna."

"I'll find out when the classes are."

"Thank you. I have work to finish and I am already too long away. Can you meet me in front of the Casa? Six o'clock? I must go home and change first, also get you your *pañuelo*. How will you get there?"

"Kenyon will drive me."

"I hope you will not feel disappointment," Esteban said.

I said, "I won't. I'll be with you."

I think that was all I cared about that summer. The war in Iraq seemed to have nothing to do with me. I'd hear my father arguing about it with Larkin. He was for it and she was very definitely against it. I was in some kind of limbo, incapable of any opinion that didn't have to do with Esteban Santiago.

FOURTEEN

I N FRONT OF THE CASA there was a tent where inside a man sold small flags and *pañuelos*. They were in boxes with labels saying Argentina, Colombia, Costa Rica, Cuba, República Dominicana, on and on. Ten dollars for the little flags; fifteen for the *pañuelos*. There were also small lapel pins for five dollars.

Esteban waited for me by the tent, his black hair parted on one side, neatly combed like his sideburns. He wore jeans and a *guayabera*, a lightweight blue cotton shirt with four pockets.

"This is my Canul Jr. Number One," he said proudly. "The other is yellow. I wear them on special occasions only."

Around his neck he wore the yellow, blue, and red–striped bandanna. I tied my *pañuelo* to my yellow belt. I was all in yellow except for the red and blue stripes in my *pañuelo*. I wore a long skirt, sandals, and a lacy blouse.

The first thing I noticed was many flags hanging above the pulpit. Esteban whispered softly, "The blue and white is Argentina. Red and white, Peru."

"Green, white, and red, Mexico," I said.

"*Sí*, Anna! You remembered." He named a few more countries that went with the flags, until it was hard to hear him.

The building was packed. I did not see anyone there I knew. While people filed by, a woman began singing *"Cristo Salva,"* a man behind her playing a bass guitar, joining in on the chorus. Then others did, and then Esteban did too. He knew all the words. He sang loudly, as though he was proud of his voice, and he held my hand

and smiled up at me.

Soon a drummer began beating time, and a pigtailed man wearing a blue and red *pañuelo* around his forehead played the electric piano.

"Remember Ramón? He's sitting behind the piano, in the *pañuelo* from Peru."

"Yes, I remember him."

"He speaks in tongues. He works for your father, too, sometimes."

Soon we could not hear each other at all, there were so many worshippers, and then suddenly we *could* hear each other, for the place became hushed, the white-and-gold curtains rustled, and a man with the same *pañuelo* Esteban and I wore came out on the stage and went up to the pulpit. His *pañuelo* was peeking from the pocket of his light-blue suit, a royal-blue shirt under the coat open at the neck. He wore a red carnation in his buttonhole. He looked very young and thin, and as he stood there with his head bowed, the roar came up from everywhere.

"AN-TO-LIN! AN-TO-LIN! AN-TO-LIN!"

It seemed so spontaneous and heartfelt, I

couldn't help feeling excited, feeling part of it, the same way sometimes a great marching band (usually one I saw on TV) would thrill me.

Antolin finally looked up, paused to regard us for a moment, then shouted a question in Spanish. Everyone stood.

I heard a microphone voice translate: "When I feel scorned, what do I do?" Hearing English, I gave Esteban a surprised look.

Then the congregation shouted back in Spanish, and the translation came again in English: "Seek God!"

"When I feel joy, what do I do?"

"Praise God!"

"When I feel depressed, what do I do?"

"Trust God!"

"When I feel at peace, what do I do?"

"Thank God!"

Everyone sat down again.

"They heard an atheist was coming," Esteban whispered in my ear. "They hired a translator so they can convert her." He took my hand and winked at me.

I closed my eyes to concentrate on the English words following Antolin's.

Antolin told of being born in Antioquia, in the rugged region of Medellin, Colombia, where orchids grew wild.

A woman called out in Spanish, "You are a wild orchid, Antolin of Antioquia." I was surprised that the translator gave the English on the microphone, and then Antolin's smiling answer.

"Our orchids grow in every color of the rainbow. Not just the lavender ones and white ones from here, but any color you can name we have at home. I miss my home as you all miss yours. I wish I could pick an orchid for every lady here today."

In the background a drum beat, then someone shook a tambourine. It was unlike any church I'd ever attended. It was a performance, and every face—black, cinnamon, brown; I saw only a few whites—every face looked relaxed and glad.

Antolin continued, waving his arms as he said, "When I came to this country, I was lonely, a sun hidden behind clouds, trying to show myself. Have you seen such a sun, ever? Yes, you have seen one and been one! All around me colors and sounds and aromas different than any I knew ever. The *gavachos* looking down on me. I was not so sure I liked them, either, and what did I miss? I missed my identity." The translator pronounced it "ideneetea."

"No one said hello to me, no one knew my name but the cold uncle who brought me here. He was a thief and not a blood relative, not a Christian, not even from Colombia. I was given to him when my family was killed by the murderers who called themselves the Heroes of the Maria Mountains. I was handed to someone who says he will become my uncle and take me to the United States of America. I thought I was blessed, but be careful when you think you are blessed, for sometimes you are used instead."

The tambourine shook again, and there was another drum roll. Somehow that was eerie, and at the same time fascinating.

Antolin went on to tell of his life in a gang

called the Barrio Kings in New York City. He told of becoming addicted to cocaine. He said one day on a fire escape, holding a pillow to muffle the sound when he broke the glass of an apartment window to burgle, he asked himself, "Is this my life? Is this how I live now? Who am I?"

Then he told of hearing Jesus tell him he was Antolin of Antioquia. "My son, He said, you are My son, and you will come to Me and find My father, for you are family."

Antolin came away from the pulpit and moved in front of it.

"We are one family. We will stick by, stand up for, love, and help each other! We are every color, not just one white field of cotton, *every* color and texture and sound and smell and WE . . . ARE . . . GOD!"

Then everyone called out in Spanish, "WE ARE GOD!"

There was a tinkling from the piano, a drumbeat, someone strummed a guitar for a second, and the tambourine was shaken.

Antolin held up his hands for silence.

"I want you to come down here"—pointing beneath him at the floor behind a gold railing— "meet me and tell me your biggest problem. Now, when we sing 'Power in the Blood,' you receive power, telling me what it is. A place to live? A doctor for the baby? A daughter who dates a *gavacho*? A beloved who is deathly ill back home, where you cannot afford to go? How will I know if you don't come and tell me before God Almighty?"

The translator did not say the English as the congregation rose and sang.

> "Hay poder, sí, sin igual poder,
> en Jesus, quien murió;
> hay poder, sí, sin igual poder,
> en la sangre que Él vertió."

Esteban whispered to me, "'There is power, power, wonder-working power, in the blood of the Lamb. There is power, power, wonder-working power in the precious blood of the Lamb.' That is what they sing now."

The music grew louder and louder, and there were some people dancing in the aisles as they formed the line for Antolin.

"Go if you want to," I said to Esteban.

"I am content sitting with you."

"But it's okay. It may be your only chance."

"No thank you, Anna."

Several people fell down, stretched out where they fell, people passing them.

"That is called *tomada del Espíritu*," Esteban said. "They are taken over by God. They have fallen in the spirit."

"Look, Esteban, there's Virgil."

He was in the line to see Antolin.

"*Sí*. Even Chino came," said Esteban.

Like some of the other men, Virgil wore a tiny black cross in one ear. The red, green, and white, the colors of Mexico, were worn like an ascot, tucked into Virgil's T-shirt, which asked "BAILAMOS?"—whatever that meant.

I thought of my strange conversation with Mitzi at the library when she'd said the ones from Ridge Road were different. I promised myself I'd call her. How often had I made that promise to myself?

It was near the very end of the service when suddenly there was no one waiting for Antolin, and the music had silenced. There was a strange, spooky sound, then a series of them, which came to my ears as something like *"Ketcho tampo ketcho tampo po po ketcho,"* and on and on.

It was not Antolin saying it. Antolin was standing back at his pulpit with his head bowed, his hands clasped in front of him in the prayer position.

The sound was coming from behind us. I turned and saw Ramón, eyes closed, hands open and held up over his head. *"Po po ket, cho po ket, cho po ket."*

"Shhhh," a woman hissed at him. "It is rude," she shouted. "It is not your service!"

Then: "Oh, but it is! It is *our* service"—from the pulpit. "Who are you, brother?"

"Ko cho pos, ah, ah, ko tampo. Ah! Ah!" I saw that Ramón was wearing a tiny black earring, too, a black cross.

"Ah! Ah! Ramón. Ramón."

"Ramón from Peru," said Antolin. "I know your colors. White, red."

"Thank you, father."

"I am not a father, Ramón. We have only one father. I am your pastor, and your brother. We are from the same family. All of us."

There was more music, and a final hymn, *"Dios os Guarde."* "God Be with You."

Finally we were crossing Montauk Highway, heading toward Esteban's Pontiac parked in the IGA lot. The moon was big and round in a gray sky, turning darker. Esteban was finding a way for us to get to the other side in heavy summer traffic.

When we were there, I asked him, "What does *gavacho* mean?"

He poked his finger near my belly. "It means you. My *gringuita.*" I remembered that word from the night of the Fourth, after the film. Ramón had used it.

Esteban smiled. "I am joking, Anna. But it means others, whites. The translator leaves out things, hmm? I'm told he is there to make English-speaking feel welcome. Townspeople complain we take over everything, even the churches."

"Not a lot of people ever went to that church, anyway, until all of you came along. And *bailamos*? What does that mean? It was written across Virgil's T-shirt."

"That is just what he had on. It means nothing. It means 'Do you want to dance?'" He grinned and took my hand. "That's what it says. Now tell me, what did you think of Antolin?"

"He was very forceful, wasn't he?"

"Yes, he was. And Antolin looks so baby-faced to have such a deep voice, did you think, Anna?"

"Yes. I liked when he said not to call him father, that he was not a father."

"*Sí.* I liked that too."

"Why were some men wearing a black cross in one ear?"

"They are brothers who accept the Blood Creed. They call themselves Blood Brothers. Ramón is leader."

"And Virgil is one?"

"He's new. Ramón has been a Blood Brother since I know him. Did you hear him speak tongues? Wasn't he fast at it?"

"Yes, he was. But those little black crosses the Blood Brothers wear freaked me out. Why black?"

"I don't know why black, Anna. I would rather wear a small gold earring," said Esteban. "My father wore one. I will get one someday." Then Esteban squeezed my hand. "You really liked being at the Casa? You are not pulling the leg?"

"I'm not pulling the leg, E.E."

"I know a place we can see the ocean in the moonlight on one side and the bay on the other."

"Are we going to Lookout Point?"

"You know that place?"

"Sure, I know it."

"But you were never there with that Trip?"

"What do you care about Trip? I love *you*!"

"I love you, too, but some say you and Trip were going steady, maybe engaged."

"We weren't, Esteban."

"Were you at Lookout Point with him?"

"No. Locals don't go to Lookout Point that much, I guess, because we can go anytime." I was more pleased that he was jealous than I was curious to know what he had heard about Trip and me, and who he had heard it from. Mitzi must have told Virgil about Trip.

"Because I would not like to go with you places you were with him," Esteban said.

"Don't worry."

"We can talk more there, where it is beautiful to see. Someday I hope we will have memories of this time when we were new. I would like those memories to be in places of great scenery. Oh Anna, I have a warm feeling."

I wanted to say, *You have the hots at last*, but there were certain times and ways I knew not to tease Esteban. He was so solemn sometimes.

"I have a warm feeling too," I said.

"I want to love you so! Do you want to love me?"

Before I could answer, a familiar battered red

Toyota barreled toward us, coming to a squealing stop as it passed us, then backing up.

"Gioconda," Esteban muttered.

"Never mind," I said. "Let's just say hello and get in your car."

But Gioconda leaned out the window, wild-eyed, yelling at Esteban in Spanish. *"Emergencia!"* she said. *"Policía!"*

He yelled back, then turned to me and said, "I have to drop you off, Anna, quickly."

"She has no right—" I began.

But Esteban took my hand and began to pull me toward his car. "Trouble!" he shouted. "Back at my house! The police are there!"

FIFTEEN

THE *SEAVIEW STAR* wrote it up this way:

RIDGE ROAD RAID

Monday evening a house at 7 Ridge Road was the scene of an eviction by Seaview police. Estimating thirty men, most of them day laborers from Latin America, Seaview authorities said they do not provide social services, so it is up to the county to help the displaced tenants.

The house was not only badly over-
crowded, but there were also multiple
safety and fire violations, including
exposed wiring and overflowing cess-
pools. The landlord, Larry Summers of
Montauk, was charging each man $300
in rent per month.

"Seaview cannot allow firetraps to
persist simply because we have an
affordable housing issue on Long
Island," veterinarian Dr. Charles Annan
said. "Seaview cannot allow immigrants to break our laws, particularly
the undocumented."

Annan himself has a home on Ridge
Road and has often complained to the
police and in the letters column of this
newspaper about conditions in the
house.

Many of the ousted tenants escaped
to the parks or woods. Others were
offered haven by Casa Pentecostal.
Pastor Luis Gomez and visiting Pastor

136

Antolin were present on Ridge Road
soon after the raid, offering emergency
shelter.

Tuesday morning word of what had happened at
Ridge Road had reached Dad's cell phone. Some
of his crew would be missing, but for once he
was more worried about his date with Larkin
than his business. As I was getting ready to leave
the house, Dad was trying on shirts—horrible
plaid polyester short-sleeved shirts. He was taking Larkin to lunch for her birthday. I couldn't
remember him ever having lunch in a restaurant.
Mom always made him lunch at home. Now he
always ordered takeout.

"Which one looks good, Annabel?" He was
beginning to go bald, so he wore this old cap
inside and out. But anyone could still see
Kenyon in his face and body. He was tall and tan
like Kenyon and I were, and he kept himself in
good shape, kayaking on Accabonac Bay, bowl-
ing and fly-fishing down at the ocean.

"They all look awful, Dad. Wear a long-sleeved

white cotton shirt with the sleeves rolled. Wear your good belt."

I was wondering if E.E. was okay, hurrying to get to the library, where I could make calls. All I knew then was that the police had raided the house on Ridge Road.

I wasn't used to seeing my dad so vulnerable. I wondered if he'd ever been nervous about what to wear on dates with my mother. I doubted it. They'd known each other since grade school, and started going steady when they both went to the same community college. Mom was never that much into clothes, either. Mostly she wore jeans and T-shirts, except Sundays at church, when she wore a skirt and heels. Not the dagger-point kind Larkin wore.

"Are my khakis all right?" Dad asked.

"They're fine. How come you're taking her to *lunch*?"

"She's making dinner for me and Kenyon. She says it's her chance to get to know him. I wish this was on another day. I'm probably short half a work crew thanks to Charlie Annan!"

"Just relax, Dad. Your face is bright red."

"Are people wearing socks anymore?"

"No one wears socks with sandals, Dad. No socks. Just your loafers. No cap. I have to go. I'll be late for work."

"You were invited to dinner too, you know."

"Larkin knows me already. I promised Mitzi I'd come over."

I felt guilty lying, and bringing Mitzi into it again. I still hadn't called her. Everything was so complicated trying to arrange times to see Esteban, and I didn't want to take on her problems with Virgil. I was curious to hear what she had to say, but at the same time I didn't want to hear her put down Latinos, particularly the poor guys from Ridge Road. I wasn't crazy about Ramón, but I had an idea a good Catholic girl like Mitzi just couldn't stand Ramón talking Virgil into leaving Holy Family.

Dad was too involved with Larkin to keep close track of me. He had never been the disciplinarian in the family, anyway. That was Mom. The funny thing is, I never would have lied to

Mom about seeing Esteban. I would have minded her, at the same time pleading my case, appealing to her as the only one who knew me. I still think she was. Mothers and daughters have something different going on than fathers and daughters.

Kenyon was waiting for me outside the library. He was angry about the raid at 7 Ridge Road, as Dad was. Kenyon disapproved of it on moral grounds. How could the city displace people with no warning, and no promise to help them find shelter? Our father feared that the eviction would permanently scare away half his work force.

"Here's the key to my place," Kenyon said. "It's an extra for Esteban, if he has no place to go."

"Thanks, Kenyon. You lock your door?" I'd forgotten that at Cornell he'd locked his dorm room door. At home we never locked up. Dad used to say all a lock did was make a burglar break your window.

"Anyone could get to the kennels from my place," Kenyon said. "Tell Esteban to remember there are valuable animals there. They *all* are to their owners."

"I don't know where Esteban and his homies are. I have to wait for his call."

"His homies," Kenyon said. "Are you going to start talking like him?"

"That's what they call each other."

"Sis . . ."

"What?"

"Never mind." He shrugged his shoulders and sank his long hands into his pants pockets. He brushed back a strand of blond hair that fell across his forehead. "Will you meet Esteban at my place when you reach him?"

"If it's all right with you."

"It's okay, I guess. . . . How involved are you with this boy?"

"How involved am I with Esteban? You're beginning to sound like Dad, Kenyon."

"Have you joined the Casa Pentecostal yet, Sis?"

"When you dropped me off there, how many whites did you see waiting out front? Did you ever think *they* might not want *me* to join *them*? You and Dad are pains in the butt, Kenyon!"

"Well, we're two guys trying to look after a motherless young girl."

"Sorry. I know you're always there for me."

"It's not easy."

"How come I suddenly need looking after?" I asked him.

"Oh, how come," he said. "How come?"

When I got inside the library, Esteban reached me. I'd left a message on his cell phone to call me there before ten. Miss Chidister usually arrived at ten fifteen in the morning.

"Anna? I would not call you at your workplace if you had not left the message on my cell."

"It's all right. We're not open yet. Where are you staying?"

"In the basement at Casa Pentecostal. I keep the furnace company."

"You can stay at Kenyon's apartment until

you find a new place."

"Tell your brother thank you, but I have Gioconda with me. And my homies, Ramón, Dario—all but Chino. We can't find Chino."

"Then at least meet me there tonight. Kenyon is going to dinner at Larkin's with my dad."

He took down the address.

"How come your homies didn't show up for work?" I asked Esteban. When I'd left the house, I'd heard my father on his cell to the crew boss asking how many they could count on.

"We let the dust settle," Esteban said.

"I don't know what you mean, E.E."

"We wait for *la migración* to get out. He called them, your fine Dr. Annan, so now you cannot anymore praise him."

"Are you sure he did?"

"We know he did. He always said he would report us to *la migra*. You see, sweet girl, many of us are undocumented."

Us. I let that sink in, and then I said, "But you're not?" My heart was suddenly beating as I waited for the answer.

"I am, Anna." Then in a singsong tone Esteban said, *"Porque no tengo papeles."* If he was trying to make light of it, for my benefit, his voice cracked as he spoke, spoiling any nonchalance.

"You have no papers?"

"That is what I am sorry to tell you, Anna."

"But you drive. How did you get a driving license?"

"Ramón knows how to get things. He is expensive, but he can get many things necessary."

I thought of Dad saying once that Latinos who did many jobs instead of one specialty often were undocumented. I knew there were many working for him, special ones he liked and had trained, but I didn't ask Dad about it. I didn't think about it. Even after I met Esteban, I didn't ask him, because why would I think he wasn't here legally?

But now I was worried for him, afraid of what could happen to him. He must have heard that in my voice, for he quickly said, "We won't discuss that stuff." He had picked up "stuff" from me. He called his belongings his "stuff," his problems "that stuff," even sometimes romance, as in the sentence, "We don't have the time or place for this stuff."

"I will be at the deli until six forty-five," he said.

"Come right after, okay?"

"I will rush to you, *cariña*. Before you become angry with me for not telling you I have no papers, I tell you now I am almost sure I can get a green card."

"I'm not angry with you, E.E."

"I prayed to Santa Cecilia for forgiveness every time I did not tell you the truth."

"What do you mean every time? Did you tell me a lot of lies?"

"I went to school to learn English so I could disguise myself, Anna, not just to get ahead. The better you speak, the less they suspect."

"I understand. You were trying to survive."

"But I *do* want to get ahead since I meet you. Anna, if I become documented, your father will not disapprove of me, *sí*?"

"I think a green card would help things."

Did Dad know Esteban was an illegal? I had no way of knowing. I didn't tell Esteban that sometimes I believed the real thing my father found wrong with him was something Esteban couldn't change. A green card wouldn't stop Dad calling him Pedro, or Juan, or José. And no matter how much more Spanish I knew in time, I would always be a *gringa*. I would always be *flour*—never *flower*.

"I will be at the address seven on time!"

"I can't wait." I couldn't. I wanted to put my arms around him and tell him everything would be okay, all the while I was thinking, *Will it be?* He could be caught and sent back to Colombia, couldn't he?

"I will see you, Anna!"

SIXTEEN

S UDDENLY I KNEW why Dr. Annan's veterinary hospital and the new Seaview Animal Shelter were both off by the airport. I could hear the dogs barking from the inside and from their runs. It made me all the more nervous, as it got to be seven-thirty, then eight, and still no Esteban.

Finally I used Kenyon's phone to call Esteban's cell.

I expected to hear him answer himself, or talk to his voicemail.

Instead, Gioconda said, "Do you think my brother is a fool, white whore?"

"No, I don't, Gioconda. May I speak with him?"

"He is working, and he will not come to that address. We know what is that address."

"It's no secret. I told him Seaview Vet."

"What trouble waits for Esteban at Dr. Annan's, Flour Face?"

I hung up.

I hadn't thought of that: Charlie Annan had been involved in the Ridge Road eviction. Had I ever told Esteban that Kenyon was staying in Charlie's garage apartment? Had I told him that would have been where he was staying if he had taken Kenyon up on the offer?

I hadn't thought of a lot of things, and neither had my brother. If Esteban had accepted my brother's offer, Charlie Annan would have intervened unless Esteban sneaked in and out. Charlie hated illegals and anyone who supported them except Dad. And *that* was a sore point between them. Esteban could never admit he stayed at Kenyon's apartment, another blow to

148

what was left of his ego.

I couldn't call Esteban at the Pantigo Deli. The only phone there was used for takeout orders, and obviously his cell was with Gioconda, probably at Casa Pentecostal, where so many were staying. He'd told me once that Gioconda did not have a job, that her job was to feed and care for everyone in the house. He said when she wasn't doing that, she was watching Cristina. I remember I thought that maybe Cristina was a small child living with them, but Esteban said Gioconda watched *El Show de Cristina Saralegui* on television; Cristina was the Latina Oprah.

I'd never find Esteban that night. When Kenyon got back, he could drive me home, but that would be hours away.

Here was my chance to call Mitzi. We used to call and e-mail each other several times a day, even when school was going and we saw each other there. I'd become a fair-weather friend, for sure. I didn't want any bad news. I didn't want to hear Esteban trashed.

"Did you hear *already*?" Mitzi said the minute she heard my voice.

"About the eviction? Everyone knows." Even though the *Seaview Star* was published on Wednesdays, the whole town was talking about Ridge Road.

"I don't mean that. I mean did you hear Virgil and I are finished? He's been avoiding me, breaking dates, that kind of thing, and finally before he went to the Casa to hear Antolin, I said, 'What's going on?' 'Nothing,' he said, 'and that's the trouble,' he said."

"What did he mean?"

"He said he doesn't feel anything for me anymore."

"Has he got another girl?"

"He said there is no one else. He said he hasn't had time to meet anyone else."

"Do you believe him?"

"Annabel, he works the same long hours your Esteban works. How could he find someone else? Besides, we've had trouble, and a big fight over something you won't believe. I don't know if

150

I can even tell you, it's so weird."

"Tell me."

"He wanted me to take an AIDS test."

"*Why?*"

"I don't know why. He couldn't tell me why. He just said everyone should take one."

"Oh, Mitz, do you think maybe *he* has AIDS?"

"I don't know what to think. And now it doesn't matter what I think. He's dumped me."

"Is there any chance you could have gotten AIDS if *he* has it?"

"Yes. But he says he does *not* have it."

I'd wondered if they were having sex, but the fact I didn't know for sure showed how much we'd lost touch. Just last year we'd bet that by the time we were seniors, we'd be the only Vestal Virgins at school. We figured most juniors and seniors at Seaview had or were having both intercourse and outercourse. Mitzi and I agreed intercourse was okay if you were really in love with a guy, but we swore we'd *never* do outercourse, even though oral sex was no big deal anymore. It *was* to us. It was too one-sided, we'd heard, too much the big male ego trip.

"I *want* to be tested now," Mitzi said, "tested for everything! But I can't go to Dr. Oliver. I'm afraid he'd tell my mother."

"Just go to Seaview Hospital. Women for Women will set up an appointment for you. Mitzi? I'll go with you if you want me to. Then we can catch up with what's going on in our lives."

"Thanks, Annabel. I'd love to have you go with me!"

"Definitely. Say when."

"I'll make an appointment. I can't talk anymore now. I'm meeting Jackie Goldman to read each other's F. Scott Fitzgerald papers. Have you done yours yet?"

"Thanks for reminding me. I almost forgot."

"I'll tell you everything when I see you."

I'd brought *Corazón Libre* with me, the Mercedes Sosa CD. I wanted to hear it with Esteban, but I played it for myself again. I'd heard it five or six times. Besides the song about the forgotten children, there was *"Todo Cambia,"* "Everything

Changes," and *"Tonada del Viejo Amor,"* "Song of an Old Love."

When Kenyon listened to her sing, he said her voice was haunting. He Googled her and found out she was in her sixties. Her voice had been compared to Billie Holiday's and Edith Piaf's. She was to Argentina what Joan Baez had been to America: a folk singer with her country as a cause.

It made me love Esteban even more, to know that was his first gift to me, and that Sosa was his mother's favorite singer. I had asked him to show me photos of his family. He said they were all back in Providencia, but he would have some sent.

Then I listened to some music Kenyon had brought there, realizing it was really from Mom's collection of old forties and fifties singers he must have transferred to CDs. Frank Sinatra, Ella Fitzgerald, Tony Bennett: the ancient sad crooners rhyming *heart* with *part* and *miss you* with *kiss you.*

Next I heard knocking on the downstairs door, and Esteban calling my name.

SEVENTEEN

"YOU LOOK *muy bella*, Anna!" He was standing in the moonlight by the garage, wearing his Canul Jr. Number Two: the yellow *guayabera* with the four pockets. It had the shine of a few hundred washes, but he had told me a *guayabera* could be worn anywhere, even to a formal dance. The writer Ernest Hemingway had worn *guayaberas*, he had told me proudly. He had his gold holy medal under it, and he had on cargo shorts. I loved his little butt and his long, thin legs, unusual for a short guy. He was grinning.

"I am late because I could not call you. I had to work late, and buses weren't running. Then your line was busy for a long time. I lent my car to Dario, and so I hitched here."

I had to laugh at myself, chiding Dad for agonizing over what to wear to Larkin's when I'd spent a long time trying things on for a date with Esteban. We weren't even going anywhere.

I'd gotten a good tan, mostly during lunch hours, when I'd walk down to Main Beach, swim, sun, and eat my lunch there.

I'd chosen white short shorts, a yellow tank top, and my boxing sneakers. Yellow because he had told me once that it was my color. I had on big hoop earrings, and I let my long blond hair hang.

Esteban came up and put his arms around me, smelling of something sweet.

"Are you wearing cologne, E.E.?" No men in our family ever wore it.

"I put on some the pastor had. Lavanda Puig eau de cologne. He said the women like it."

"It's sweet, like you, E.E."

He had to stand on tiptoe to kiss me. He whispered, "I missed you."

"I called you and got Gioconda."

"She read the address here and said it was a trap."

"Doesn't she know I would never hurt you, that I love you?"

"Was she nasty, Anna?"

"Of course not! Gioconda? She was her old, sweet self."

"You make fun with me."

I could tell he was in a loving mood, and he was getting me in one too. We couldn't keep our hands off each other.

"Hey," I said. "Don't you think we should go upstairs?"

"Are you sure there are no policemen sent from Dr. Annan?" He laughed and I punched his arm. And we kissed. And we kissed.

I said, "Are your toes tired?" The minute I said it, I was afraid he might be offended because I'd referred to his height, but he was so easy, so ready to smile and laugh and hold me.

He said, "Sí. My *dedos del pies* need rest. You know what I love, Anna?"

"What?"

"That you make no fuss because I have no papers. I thought you would maybe tell me *adiós* when you found that out. It has happened to my homies more than once. Nobody likes you when you have no papers."

"Come on," I said. "Follow me."

We walked hand in hand to the back door of the garage. He was telling me it took him a long time to get a ride there. Dario had borrowed the Pontiac to pick up some of the homies still hiding in the woods.

Esteban's hands were as rough as his face, and his shoulders and arms were soft. Next time I would bring my Nivea cream and massage his fingers and palms.

We climbed the outside stairs, my heart pounding, his too, I bet, and we were laughing a little at nothing, at being with each other.

Besides the Lavanda Puig there was the aroma of dog from the kennels, one I liked, but I asked Esteban, "Does the dog perfume clash with your cologne?"

He giggled and said, *"Un poco."*

Then I said, "What's wrong with this door?"

"I'll try it, Anna."

"You won't get in, I'm afraid."

I had locked us out. The keys were inside.

"What have you done?" he said, and we began to laugh again, at my stupidity, at the two of us champing at the bit to be somewhere with our arms and legs around each other, standing instead on the stairs.

"Of all times to be without my car," Esteban said. "I cannot even take us somewhere away."

"Let's go downstairs, sit on the bench out front, and think about this."

"Maybe we should hitch to Main Beach," he said.

I didn't want to believe we were locked out, and I remembered Kenyon's penchant for hiding keys to his room in college. He had one of those tiny black magnet boxes, and he would attach it to the sides of stairs, to the overhead on his door, anywhere and everywhere. Maybe he did the same thing here. Even though he'd given me my own key, he might have kept a secret key for himself, in case he got locked out.

The night sky was filled with stars and an enormous moon.

"The beach?" Esteban said. We were always there. It was okay because he brought along his boom box and we danced on the boardwalk. He was teaching me the neotango. But there were always kids from school chilling there, and I didn't like them talking about me. One look at Esteban and me, and they knew we were in love. I imagined them whispering behind their hands. There were a few other girls dating Latinos, but the ones from my class were dating Latinos from school, not ones who were just here to work. I'd been telling myself that once Dad got past his thing against Esteban, I wouldn't care who saw us or what anyone said. But it wasn't that easy, particularly now that I knew he was undocumented.

There was a different feeling about the workers. I was always the good girl, admiring the ones who were rebels but never tempted to go Goth or run with the cutters or the loose gooses.

"Let me go back up there and take one last look, E.E. I have an idea he might have hidden a key."

"Look, Anna." He pointed up at the moon. "*La luna nueva*. Do you know it brings luck?"

"I hope so! I'll be right back," I said. "Don't go away."

I had this giddy, high feeling that seemed to be there whenever Esteban was. I remember Mom saying she had a chemistry with Dad, that if *that* wasn't there nothing could make it appear: not money, not looks, not occupation; it was just this *thing* you had with only one person. It happened right away, she said, *bang!* Kenyon was taking French at Seaview High then. He said the French called it *coup de foudre*. A thunderbolt, a gunshot: That was what it was first time I laid eyes on E.E.: *Bang!*

I didn't hear anyone drive up, but from the

160

top of the stairs, outside Kenyon's door, I heard a man shouting down in the yard, and soon after the sounds of fighting.

I went down the stairs as fast as I could and collided at the bottom with Dr. Annan.

He was out of breath, holding his hand over his chin as he reached inside the garage and turned on the overhead light.

Esteban was nowhere in sight.

"Someone was just trying to break in. Did you hear anything?" he asked me.

"I was taking a look at Kenyon's apartment when I heard something that sounded like a fight."

"I got a punch thrown at me. I saw this kid when I drove up, Latino kid hanging around here. I called out, 'What the hell do you want here?' I even left my car lights on while I tried to get him, but he got me first."

"I didn't see anyone," I said. It was then that I noticed he had the Santa Cecilia medal in his hand, the gold chain broken.

Dr. Annan said, "I'm glad for your sake I had

to come by. Who knows what that spic wanted around here?"

"Are you sure he was a Latino?"

"Could have been one of them from Ridge Road, getting even. Little guy. Big fist."

Charlie Annan had on jeans and a black T-shirt that read WE CARE FOR YOUR CRITTERS. He was a tall, good-looking man, a redhead with blue eyes and freckles, boyish looking, but I knew he was about ten years younger than my father. While he opened his car door and turned off the lights, he kept rubbing his chin where Esteban must have hit him.

"Good thing there was this emergency, Annabel," Charlie said.

"What emergency, Doctor?"

"Dalí was run over in front of Larkin's. They called me, and I told them to meet me here." I saw him shove Esteban's medal into his jeans.

"Well, they've arrived," I said, watching Dad's truck turn in.

I was surprised that Esteban had been able to reach Charlie Annan's chin, and glad he got away.

"I'll find a way to get your medal back. I know it was lucky for you."

"Like the new moon, huh? Some luck, Anna. Well, is Dalí okay? I prayed to San Antonio for him. San Antonio de Padua. He cares for sick family members and distressed animals."

I was always surprised when Esteban spoke of praying. Even though I knew my father and Kenyon probably prayed, I never thought of them that way unless they were in church.

"Dalí's wearing a cast. The doctor's really not a bad man, Esteban."

"I'm really not a spic, either."

"My father sometimes uses that language, too," I told him, "but he doesn't mean to offend anyone. He's just from the old school. They don't know how offensive it is."

Esteban said, "They know better, the same way they know to hire men who'll work for nothing. They claim we do work no white man will do, but that is a lie! What is truth is no white man will work for what we are paid!" He pulled me close to him and said, "I don't hold you responsible for what your father or Charlie Annan do. We're our own society. You. Me."

I thought of that preacher at Casa Pentecostal saying, "We are God."

The soccer players were calling his name.

"They don't need me," he said.

"Play," I said. "You need them."

He held me away from himself for a second and smiled. He looked at me as though I was this wise, wise babe, knowing him better than he knew himself. All I really had to know was that soccer was part of our society. Esteban. Me. Soccer.

That was all right with me.

I'd watch.

When it got dark, the cars turned their headlights on and parked circling the field, so the teams could finish the match. Esteban told me to go home, that after the game he would not have time to be with me anyway. He had to try and find Chino, who was still missing after the eviction. Rumors were he was camping on an ocean beach, terrified because years ago the INS had

166

sent his brother home where living conditions were dangerous. Some Colombians were simply disappearing forever.

I went home to find Dad waiting for me, sitting in the screening room watching some old baseball game on TV. He was wearing shorts, which he never wore around Larkin, and a T-shirt saying SUPPORT OUR TROOPS. Dad never wore that around Larkin either. Larkin had been against the Iraq war before it started, and when Dad said he was, too, but he supported our boys, Larkin would get angry. She'd say if he was *for* them, he'd get them out of there before they were all dead. It was a subject both of them avoided after one shouting match that sent Larkin into the night crying.

My father said, "What are you pulling, Annabel? If you're not coming home for dinner, how about calling?"

"I didn't think we were back having dinner every night at seven," I said. "Half the time you go to Larkin's."

"And I let you know. Ahead of time."

"Yes, you do. It's hard when I don't have a cell phone."

"All right, you can have it back. I'm trusting you've come to your senses about Pedro."

"Esteban."

Dad shrugged. "Whatever. He was living there in that Ridge Road rat house, you know."

"How would I know that?"

"I'm telling you. That was the address I had for Dario. *And* Ramón. When I went down there that Saturday morning to find your *friend*" (he said the word with as much sarcasm as he could manage), "they all came out like cockroaches in the light."

"Maybe with what they get paid, they can't afford our big rents."

Dad picked up the remote control and turned the set off.

"Annabel, they were all paying some landlord from Montauk $300 each a month. So their landlord was getting about $9000 a month in rent. Why don't those boys put their Juan Does on a mortgage? Why don't they *buy* a place?"

"I don't know why, Dad." I knew why. I think Dad did, too. How could they go through bank inspections and all the legal entanglements without papers?

I had made up my mind that soon I would talk with Dad about Esteban. I would ask him to let me make dinner for us, with Larkin there. If Dad could just get to know Esteban, I believed, he would not be so dead set against him.

I wanted to plan it. I had to be sure of the timing. It couldn't be an evening like this one, with Larkin worried about Dalí and refusing to leave his side. That didn't go over very big with Dad, who never fancied anything on four legs being featured over him, even if one of the legs was in a cast.

I had an idea that Larkin would help me, too, at the right time. She was a romantic, for sure. I think that really appealed to Dad. Mom and he had become like old shoes, used to each other for years and years. Loving, yes, chemistry, I suppose . . . but no visible sparks.

I couldn't remember Mom ever really flirting

with Dad. Larkin was always on around him, touching him, calling him her pet names (Kenny was inevitable, I suppose, but Dear Ears? Tootsie Roll? Beauty Guy?). It was a nice gift for Dad, this vamp landing in his life suddenly, making him worry about wearing the wrong shirt or pants.

"I suppose a lot of them are illegals. Of course *I* hire illegals," Dad continued. "Sure, *some* are illegal, but I don't ask."

"You're not supposed to." I remembered that from Current Events class. Employers couldn't ask about race, religion, national origin, sexual orientation, pregnancy status, or disability.

"I wouldn't ask anyway," Dad said. "I'm only interested in having them work and stick around. It's business, that's all it is. Business is business."

"Well, the landlord from Montauk is in business, too." I was sorry I said it. Dad was ready for an argument. I knew that the second he told me Larkin couldn't see him that night because Dalí needed her. Dad had now turned his back on the

TV. He was headed toward the refrigerator, dropping an empty beer bottle into the garbage can by the stove.

He said, "Annabel, I wouldn't be in that kind of business—taking advantage of people. I pay my *muchachos* a decent salary. Some of them are raising families on what I pay them, sending money home with some left over. But I'll tell you something, Annabel, people who are taken advantage of are often people who take advantage, if you know what I mean." *Pop!* Another beer bottle top hit the dust.

I said, "I'm beat, Dad. I'm going up to bed and watch a *Seinfeld* rerun."

"*I* like *Seinfeld*," he said.

"I want to be in bed when I watch it."

I knew he was going to make me feel guilty, leaving him alone that way.

I knew he knew it, and he'd make a joke so I wouldn't feel bad.

"Leave your old man to cry in his beer," he said.

Thank heaven the phone rang. It was Larkin,

because after Dad said Hello, he gave me a wave and then carried the phone down the length of the room, to the couch.

I couldn't help remembering being on that couch with Esteban under me, calling him Swan Man, smelling his sweat and his sweet breath, neither of us at that moment knowing there were nails in our future, too.

"I was just watching *Masterplace Theater*," I heard Dad say. How was he supposed to know it was *Master*piece *Theater*, that it was never on in summer, and that it was too late to be on, anyway?

NINETEEN

"**G**ET IN," KENYON SAID. He was waiting for me in front of the library, driving a new Cooper. Red with the white top down. His graduation gift from Dad. I'd promised I wouldn't drive until I was eighteen, even though I could have gotten a junior license.

If *I* wasn't out on the road, Dad said, that meant one less worry for him. If I kept my promise, said Dad, we'd talk about a secondhand car he'd get me for summers and vacations from college.

Kenyon said, "Dad and Larkin are going out for a lobster dinner, so I thought we could go for a fish fry. Are you free?"

"Yes, Esteban's working." I got into the front seat.

"Is he your whole life now or something?"

"Sure, Kenyon. He's my whole life. I'm never without him."

"You don't have to be so sarcastic."

"Do you realize how little time Esteban and I have together?"

"I think stolen moments make a new relationship all the more intense," Kenyon said. "Maybe if you could see him every night the way you did Trip, he wouldn't be—"

I didn't let him finish. "I didn't see Trip every night. I saw Trip every night he decided we'd see each other. He wasn't in love with me, and now I know I wasn't in love with him, either. I was in love with his boat, his car, the restaurants we could afford to go to—all the superficial stuff."

"Don't you miss any of that, Sis?"

"I don't yet."

"That's an honest answer. I was hoping we could discuss this without me saying something gross or something that would make you angry."

"Why?"

"Because I know you can tell me things you can't tell Dad. Remember, Sis, I'm part of the team looking out for you. Mom would want that. She'd want me to make sure you're not getting in over your head."

"I'm trying not to. It's different, though, with Esteban. He's not Trip. He's not like any boy I've ever dated. He really feels the same way I feel about him."

Kenyon looked so handsome, tall and tan, wearing white shorts, a red T, and a Yankees cap. I had the thought that we looked like some steady couple off for an evening of fun, in a convertible where everyone could see us. How long had it been since that had happened? Maybe I did miss that life a little bit, but what I had with Esteban was unique. I had never seen someone look at me the way he did. I had never felt myself tremble when he just strolled toward me with that look in his eyes.

Kenyon said, "Since we're on the subject of Esteban, Sis, I have to tell you something. I can't offer my apartment to Esteban anymore. If Charlie found out, he'd be mad as hell at me for helping a Latino, and also for keeping you and Esteban secret from Dad. It'd all come out."

"I know. I thought of that. Sometimes I think I should just marry Esteban. I'll be eighteen next winter. He'd be a citizen automatically, and if we were married, Dad would have to accept him."

"*Marry* him?"

"Don't get excited. That just popped into my head from nowhere. We've never talked about getting married."

"I hope not. That would be a sure way to get him deported if he has no papers. He probably doesn't."

"Kenyon, I'm not serious."

"But be serious about what can happen to your Esteban if he needs identification for *any* reason."

"He hasn't any papers. He's very vulnerable, isn't he?"

"*Very*, honey. There's something else." He sighed. He said, "Charlie's afraid there's some Ridge Road revenge in the cards because of coming upon Esteban a few weeks ago."

"He has no idea who it was, Kenyon."

"But he thinks it was someone from Ridge Road trying to get even. Now he's stirring things up trying to defeat the hiring hall. That could be trouble too. That's one issue Dad and he don't see eye to eye on at all!"

In Seaview a lot of people were sick of seeing Latinos waiting for jobs down by the railroad station. They wanted them to be in a hiring hall. There was a plan to buy the old police station and turn it into a place where they could congregate, where there were rest rooms and where they weren't conspicuous. Of course, Charlie Annan opposed it. He didn't want to encourage Latinos to live in Seaview at all. There were plenty of people who agreed with him. Dad didn't, because he needed Latinos to stay in business.

"Charlie Annan had that idea way before anything happened at Ridge Road," I said.

"I know he did. But he's really going to push it now. So Dad and Charlie are going to be at odds," said Kenyon. "I just thought you ought to know. Not that there's anything anyone can do about it." He looked across at me and smiled. "Hey, let's put this behind us and have a fun evening."

"There's just one thing. Can you get Esteban's holy medal back, Kenyon? Charlie grabbed it when they fought."

"If there was any way I could, I would. But how would I do that?" Kenyon said.

He drove out to Fish Eddy's on the highway near Montauk. We took our food to Lookout Point and ate dinner watching the kayaks in the bay on one side, and the huge ocean waves on the other. Kenyon said he knew it was corny to park there, that not many locals did, but it was the one view he'd longed for when he was back at Cornell during one of upstate New York's winters.

I told Kenyon my plan to have Esteban to dinner one night.

Humongous sigh.

"Good luck!" he said.

"You don't have to come. Just Larkin and me and Dad."

"I said, good luck!"

"You aren't really cheering me and Esteban on, are you?"

"It's just so much trouble to go through," Kenyon said. "He's unskilled and undocumented."

"All of which can be fixed with time," I said.

"And if it *can* be fixed, what happens then? You don't even look at the college catalogs anymore. I see they're piled up in the hall at home."

"When school's out, it's hard for me to think about college. I need people around me who are thinking about college."

"No danger of that now," Kenyon said sarcastically. "Even if he can become legal, what does that mean to the two of you?"

"I don't know, Kenyon. I just know we have

this chemistry. Right from the start we've had it. Remember you taught Mom and me *coup de foudre*?"

"Mom wasn't talking about someone from South America nobody knows anything about! Anna B., he may be a great guy; he probably is. But what I'm concerned about is *you*. You're getting into something with someone who isn't accountable. He could be here today and gone tomorrow. Where would that leave you?"

"He's accountable. He is unless your boss sics Immigration on him."

"Well, that's Charlie's bugaboo. He's a little crazy on the subject. Yesterday he told me he was composing a petition to stop the library from buying books in Spanish. He said taxpayer money shouldn't be spent on anything that promotes languages other than English."

"How do you stand him?"

"He's a very skilled vet, Annabel. He can do surgery a lot of New York doctors don't know how to do. And he's an old friend of our family's."

Who wanted to hear accolades for Charlie

God-awful Annan? Change the subject, Anna B.

I said, "Kenyon? Mom would like Esteban!"

"What would she like about him, Sis?"

"He's a believer. She'd like that. He says without God life doesn't make sense. I don't ever ask him what sense it makes *with* God."

"Don't start on that subject," Kenyon said. "Tell me what else Mom would like about Esteban."

"Give me time to think."

"You brought it up. I imagined you'd given it some thought. You don't even know him, Sis."

"I'm trying to get to know him. It's not easy with both my father and my brother down on him."

"I'm not down on him, Sis. And Dad is clueless about you two. His head is in the clouds, thanks to Larkin. I see he returned your cell phone."

"Yes, I have it back. Kenyon? Wait until *you* fall for someone," I said. "I don't think you've ever been in love."

"I already have fallen for someone," Kenyon

said. "Her name is Maxine, and she'll be staying with me for a week, in two weeks."

When I got home later, Larkin was watching an HBO movie about Jackson Pollack, the abstract artist who put his canvas on the floor and threw paint at it.

She turned it off, and I said, "Larkin, keep watching it. I'll watch with you."

"I've seen it, Annabel. Poor Pollack. Do you know, before he was famous, *Life* magazine called him Jack the Dripper."

"At least he got into *Life* magazine," I said.

"That was his beginning."

Dad was at the kitchen counter on the phone, handling a work emergency, trying to get a crew together for a new job. Even weeks later he was still missing fellows from Ridge Road. Some had left Seaview and some were relocating to a house down near the train station. Esteban was planning to relocate there too.

Dalí was up on the couch, his cast finally off,

wagging his tail because I'd entered the screening room.

I thought of telling Larkin that it was Esteban at Dr. Annan's that night, but I still wasn't sure yet how much she told Dad. I didn't want to get Kenyon in trouble, either.

"Poor Kenny can't ever relax," Larkin said. "Do you ever cook dinner, Annabel?"

"I cook a few things. Dad likes my meat loaf." (Of course—Mom's recipe.) "Has he complained that I don't cook?"

"No. Your father has nothing but praise for you. It's my idea that he should come home to a good meal at night. I'd do it if there was any way I could, but I'm mounting a show now."

"We've always managed, Larkin."

"He's never been so stressed, though. Now there are rumors Dr. Annan is causing more trouble."

"Kenyon says he wants the library to stop buying books in Spanish," I said. "And he's back opposing the hiring hall."

"Poor Charlie. Sometimes perfectly nice people get these fixations. Your father says Charlie needs a woman."

Larkin was wearing a white skirt with a backless green blouse and high-heeled white sandals. She was drinking a bottle of Stewart's low-calorie root beer with a straw.

"I'm still seeing him," I said in a whisper. I didn't need to whisper. Dad was barking into his cell down at the other end of the room.

"I had an idea you were," she said.

"I can't help it, Larkin."

"I know, Annabel. I do know."

"I don't like sneaking around. Do you think I could have him to dinner with you and Dad?"

"Well . . . why not?" she said.

"Do you *mean* it, Larkin?"

"I mean it, Annabel. But don't expect a miracle."

"Meaning?"

"Your father isn't against Esteban because there's anything wrong with the young man. Kenny's *afraid*, Annabel. He thinks he could lose you. I remember when I wanted to go to UCLA to study, years ago, my father was upset because he thought I'd fall in love with someone from California. He was afraid I'd spend all my holidays across the country in California, because wives went home with their husbands then."

"Times have changed, Larkin. We're not that sexist anymore."

"We're not that changed, either. Oh, honey, Kenny is probably never going to approve of Esteban. He comes with too much baggage."

"Will you help me? I think if he came to dinner and Dad could hear him talk about music and films and his own home, Providencia, he'd see he's not that different from guys around here."

Larkin said, "Guys around here *live* around here. It's that simple. This boy lives in the wrong place. What kind of a future do you envision with him, honey?"

"I don't envision anything but having him come to dinner."

"Your father says you used to have your

friends over a lot, but now you don't."

"Well? I have to sneak around to see him. If Dad approved of him, I wouldn't have to sneak around."

At least I'd go with Mitzi for her appointment at Seaview Hospital, in ten days. She said we'd have a lot to talk about when she saw me. She'd tell me everything.

"If you want to have him to dinner, Annabel, Kenny and I will be here. You name the date."

"Thanks, Larkin!"

Dalí picked up my excitement, jumped up, and began licking me, wagging his tail, his nails scratching my bare legs.

Larkin said, "Down, Dalí!" She turned back to me and said, "Maybe it would be a good idea just to say you're having a little dinner party, and we're invited. You don't have to tell Kenny that Esteban is coming."

"You're learning, aren't you?" I said.

We both laughed.

"Wait! I have an idea," said Larkin. "Let's have Kenyon's new girlfriend to dinner too. She's coming here soon, and she'll take the spotlight off anyone because of what she does."

"What does she do?"

"Hasn't Kenyon told you?"

"He hasn't said much about her at all."

"She runs Green Pastures," Larkin said. "That's the new environmental kind of cemetery. It's located down the island. You'd never know it's a cemetery, but it is. Green Pastures specializes in green burial."

"The kind without a coffin? I read something about it somewhere."

"Without embalming, without a coffin: The body just goes, *pffft*, into a hole in the ground. That's her profession."

"You're right," I said. "That would take the spotlight off anyone."

TWENTY

"A MERICANS ARE THE only ones who ever embalmed the dead," Maxine said. "We started doing it during the Civil War because we had all these dead soldiers to transport all over the country. They wouldn't hold together if they weren't preserved somehow."

Larkin said, "You two are my witnesses. When I die, I want to go to Green Pastures."

"Me too," I said.

It was Larkin's idea to have two pitchers of

sangria, one without booze in it for Esteban, me, and anyone else who would not be drinking that night, and one pitcher of what she called *"real"* sangria. That one had rum and brandy in it.

Maxine said, "*Real* for me, thanks."

"Good. Then I have company," said Larkin. "Kenny won't drink sangria. He calls it 'punch.' He says it ruins both the fruit and the liquor."

"I'm already afraid of him," Maxine said. "Kenyon makes him sound so formidable."

"He's not," Larkin said.

"He's not with you," I said.

While she filled their glasses, Maxine wandered around looking over the screening room. She was tall, with sun-blond hair that spilled to her shoulders but did not hide the tattoo near her shoulder bone. It was a lot of straight red lines. She told us it was a Kanji character for truth, which reminded me of Diogenes, the famous Greek philosopher who was out with his lantern in the daylight, searching for an honest man. I'd done a paper on him for history. He scorned material things and lived in a tub.

I'd received an A for that paper. School seemed so far away now, yet we'd be back there in a few weeks.

Maxine wore a Levi's maxi skirt with a pale-blue short-sleeved tunic, and red lace-up sneakers with white toes and white shoestrings.

Kenyon had warned Larkin and me that Maxine didn't eat meat or chicken, and that she stepped outside now and then to smoke a beadie, an herbal cigarette. He'd never told me what she did for a living. That hurt my feelings a little, because how could he talk about her with Larkin but not me?

Esteban was bringing a large paella as soon as he finished work at six. I'd asked him to make one without sausage or chicken, to fill it instead with lobster, shrimp, clams, mussels, pimiento, green peas, and saffron rice.

Dad, who had no clue Esteban would be there, was arriving late. Another job emergency.

Kenyon was outside showering.

Larkin said, "This is the best part of a mixed-sex evening, you know, when we females get to be alone. It usually happens after dinner, but I like it before. We have a chance to talk."

"I'm too nervous to be at my best," I said. I knew Kenyon had told Maxine this was a dinner so Dad could meet both her and Esteban.

"So let me get this straight," said Larkin, carrying her drink over to the couch. "Someone dies. The body goes to Green Pastures. It's put as is into a shroud. Then you take it to a field where there's a hole dug, and you drop it into the hole?"

Maxine sat beside her on the couch while I took the ottoman opposite them.

"We don't use the word *shroud*," Maxine said. "We call it a *linceul*, which is French for 'shroud.'"

"That sounds so much lighter," Larkin said.

"Exactly," said Maxine. "We try to take the old spookiness out of death."

"Who's *we*?" I asked.

"Me and my ex," Maxine said. "We met at Cornell, and we always thought we'd get married after graduation. But he discovered he was gay."

"The Gay Undertaker," said Larkin.

"Neither of us are undertakers."

"I was just kidding," said Larkin. "But if you don't call yourselves undertakers, what do you call yourselves?"

"Facilitators. And we don't call the hole 'the hole.' We call it 'the opening.'" Maxine took a sip of her drink. I noticed another Kanji character tattooed on her wrist, green lines and boxes. "We have twenty acres. You would drive by and think it was a woods with lanes and park benches, but no gravestones. Just a tiny nameplate horizontal with the ground. Underneath, everything blends together and feeds what's above."

"No one knows it's a cemetery?"

"One might know, but not because there are any outside signs, except the ones saying 'Private. Green Acres.'"

Esteban arrived before Dad. He had washed and ironed the blue *guayabera*, which he wore with jeans and sneakers. (He told me once he liked to iron.) I helped him carry the Pantigo Deli bags from his car to the mini kitchen in the screening room.

"I am back living at the Casa," he said softly

to me. "Only the documented can live in the new place."

"Did you remember no chicken or meat?"

"Of course. Do you even *listen* to me, Anna?"

"I'm sorry. I heard you. I'm just nervous."

"I am not nervous," said Esteban. "If your father cannot stand me, how can *I* stand *him* and have my self-respect?"

"Later, Swan Man. We'll talk later." I kept forgetting to ask him what he knew about Virgil and Mitzi breaking up, and why Virgil wanted her to be tested for AIDS.

After we got the food in the oven, Esteban put his hands behind his back and said, "Guess which one has something for you, *cariña*."

I made a guess and he produced another CD. There was a gorgeous blonde looking over her shoulder, which had the tattoo "Laundry Service" high on one arm. Down the side of "Laundry Service" was her name: Shakira.

"Ah! The famous Shakira! I want to hear her with you."

"Of course!"

"We can listen to her later," Esteban said. "My favorite song of hers is on this CD. 'Whenever, Wherever.' You will like it, Anna. It is a song for us. You'll see."

"Thanks, E.E. You mustn't keep buying me gifts."

"I feel I must." He reached up to kiss me. "*Te amo.*"

"*Te amo,* E.E."

Then we went down into the screening room, where Esteban swooned over Larkin's three-legged table. He told Larkin he had great respect for artists, that he had never met one "in person," that the creative people he knew were all musicians.

"Where do you paint?" he asked.

"I have a studio in my house. Someday you can visit it."

"I would be so honored."

"Sometimes I need someone to put large canvases in my van, or help stretch them. You could make some extra money."

Esteban shook his head and held his hands up. "No! No! No pay! I don't need money!"

How proud he was! He would never let me pay for anything. I did my best to think of things we could do that wouldn't cost money. Esteban worked every opportunity he could, because his family in Colombia depended on the money he sent. He told me that if he failed to send it, it could mean they would be put out of their house, they could even go hungry. They counted on what he sent to live. The little gifts he was always giving me he afforded by working extra hours and not buying things for himself.

Enter Kenneth Brown.

"Hello, everyone!"

"Hello, Kenny sweet-soul!" Larkin cried out. She ran to him, and they did one of those French-style greetings Dad used to complain about, complicated cheek kissing, one side first, then the other, instigated by Larkin.

Dad stood in the center of the room punching his left palm with his right fist, then the right one with the left. He was wearing his old khakis, white socks, Nikes, a navy T-shirt, and his old cap that said BROWN ALL OVER TOWN.

"Mr. Brown?" said Maxine, heading his way with outstretched hand. "I'm Kenyon's friend, Maxine Segelkin."

They were shaking hands when suddenly Esteban stepped forward. "Mr. Brown? I'm Annabel's friend, Esteban Santiago."

Dad actually grabbed his outstretched hand and shook it. He said, "Maybe I should nickname you Nails Santiago." Big ha ha ha from Dad.

Esteban gave a little bow. Unsmiling.

"I hope you brought some of that *pie-ella*," said Dad.

"Yes, sir, I brought *pie-yea-ya*."

"Hail, hail, the gang's all here," said Dad, and I wasn't sure if he was being sarcastic or trying to be funny.

Then he said he was going to change clothes.

Staring a moment at Maxine, Dad said, "There's a green smudge on your wrist, honey."

"It's a tattoo," she said, smiling with her great white teeth and, yes, dimples. "It's a Kanji character for hope. Someone once said death is the greatest evil, because it cuts off hope."

"That is a good saying," Esteban said. "I will memorize that."

My father looked at them a moment, gave them one of his now-you-see-it-now-you-don't smiles, and went on into the house. When he passed me the expression on his face said, *Say what?*

I wasn't sure if he meant the tattoo or Esteban.

TWENTY-ONE

THE DINNER DISCUSSION, of course, centered on green burial. My father usually fought the idea of anything new, growling when he first heard of something that no one *needed:* television in color, an electric typewriter, a computer, a cell phone—all of those things, he'd often proclaimed, were just a way to milk the public. Now he had all of those things.

I was amazed when his eyes lit up as Maxine described Green Pastures, and when he exclaimed, "Book me in! Can I pay for a hole in advance?"

"We call them 'openings'," said Maxine. "And we do arrange for pre-need."

"Arrange an opening for my opening." Dad guffawed at his own joke.

Kenyon, his hair still wet from the shower, his eyes shining when he looked across the table at Maxine, said he wouldn't mind having one too.

"Mom would approve of this," he said. "She was a conservationist, remember. And an environmentalist. This way, the land stays the land. It doesn't fill up with a lot of headstones."

He was right about Mom. Dad used to tease her, saying she was a "tree hugger." My mother would have approved of Maxine's green burial. She'd believed in God but not an afterlife. Dead was dead, she believed, same as I did. She'd been cremated and told us not to ask for her ashes. The whole idea of that gave her the creeps.

I looked across at Esteban. He said very little, except to answer questions Kenyon was polite enough to ask him, when Kenyon noticed he wasn't talking. What position do you like to play in soccer? (Goalie.) How long have you been in the United States? (Two years.) Why did you choose Seaview? (Gioconda came first to manage a house of immigrants. She told Esteban how wonderful it was here.) That sort of thing. Then came the point when Esteban said something softly to Larkin, and she poured real sangria into his empty water glass.

I'd never known Esteban to drink. He said he didn't like the smell or the taste of alcohol. I knew he was feeling the strain of trying to fit in where he didn't fit in.

"Good. Very good," he said.

"Too strong?" Larkin asked.

"Just right."

Esteban ate with his right hand, and rubbed near his neck with his left. It was a reflex action; he always used to touch his holy medal when he was nervous. When his eyes looked up at mine, he almost smiled, his expression saying to me something like *Don't worry, Anna, I'm okay*. I thought he looked adorable with that upper right tooth a little crooked.

Maxine was telling us the bodies were buried vertically, in a fetal position.

"Then you take up less land," said Dad.

"I think one should be buried in a casket," said Esteban.

Larkin was following Dad's conversation. "A fetal position! You go out the way you came in."

"That's a good slogan," said Kenyon. "'Go out as you came in.'"

Esteban said again, "I believe one should be buried in a casket. There could be worms in the soil."

Silence. Was I the only one who had heard him?

No, Dad had heard him. Dad sang, "The worms crawl in, the worms crawl out," and he chuckled to himself.

Esteban frowned, put down his fork, shoved his plate away, then pulled it back in front of him, as though he'd realized it was a rude gesture. But he didn't eat.

"Speaking of going out," Maxine said, pushing

back her chair, "excuse me."

While she walked to the door, Kenyon said, "She smokes."

Dad said to me, "I left some mail on your bed, honey. There's a catalog from the Jane Addams School of Social Work."

"Thanks, Dad."

"Or do you still like Simmons College?"

"I don't know, Dad."

"Chicago or Boston. Which city appeals to you?"

"I haven't given it much thought," I said.

"Boston's closer to home," he said. "And there are all those Harvard boys in Boston."

Thanks, Dad!

I wished he wouldn't start on college. In a week I'd be back at Seaview High. Everyone I knew would be talking about college then, getting ready to take their SATs, going off with their folks to see various campuses, everything that would begin to distance Esteban and me. He'd sometimes ask me about college, what I would study, if I would go someplace near, if I would want to see him once I was there. But we both knew it was a minefield; we knew not to walk in that direction for very long.

Dad finally turned to Esteban. "Where are you boys living now?"

"Some of us are living in a new house and some of us are at Casa Pentecostal. I'm staying at the Casa."

"But you're moving into the new house," I said.

"When I came in, Anna, I told you I cannot stay there."

My father said, "But that's nice of the pastor to take you in there temporarily. You religious?"

"Yes, sir."

"You go to Holy Family?"

"Here in America I go to Casa Pentecostal."

"I can see why," said Dad. "Does the pastor charge you rent?"

"No. I don't plan to stay there."

"Where *do* you plan to stay?"

"I am at work on that."

"I guess there are a load of uncertainties in your life, hmm?"

"Yes, sir," said Esteban. "Not so many I can't handle them."

Good! Show your mettle, E.E.

"You didn't handle them all that well down on Ridge Road," said Dad.

"We were working too hard. You know how that is, sir, we got too busy to pay attention to what was going on at the house."

"Yes, I do know what that's like," said Dad.

They were having this little word duel when Larkin very dramatically sailed her napkin to her plate and said, "I ate so much I need fresh air, and I have to walk Dalí."

"I'll walk him," I said.

"I will go with you," said Esteban.

"Thanks," said Larkin. "I'll take the dishes away."

"Let me help, Larkin," Kenyon said.

Dad always knew how to clear a room.

TWENTY-TWO

B Y THE TIME we got Dalí outside, Maxine was on her way back in.

"Wait!" I said to Esteban when he tried to pull me close. "Let the poor dog pee first."

I could smell the Lavanda Puig cologne. I hoped Dad couldn't. He always said he wouldn't go into the Accabonac General Store mornings for coffee, because all the truckers wore after-shave and stank like hookers.

When Dalí was finished, I tied his leash to the

porch railing and held my arms out to Esteban.

After a while we could talk.

"How are you doing, Swan Man?"

"You are the only one in the wide world I would do this for, Anna."

"I didn't know all the details of Maxine's business. That was news to me."

"I find Maxine okay."

"All that talk of death didn't bother you?"

"I can see it might bother you. It made me regret we could never put Papi in a grave. There was no Papi at the end, just the *grito de mi madre*. A neighbor come to Mami where she was sweeping the sidewalk in front and said they have taken him. I still hear her scream."

"How old were you?"

"Six."

"I'm so sorry, Esteban."

"When she told me he was gone, for a while I was glad. He was not an easy parent. When he came home, no matter day or night, no matter who was watching television or if they were in the middle of a *telenovela*, he switched channels to what he wanted. It was always what he wanted in everything! It took me a while to appreciate he really was gone. Forever. Then it took me a while to realize how I had loved him. He worked so hard for us, Anna. Our lives would never be the same without him. I cried all the time for a whole year. Then when I was old enough, I followed his example and became a support for my *familia*."

"I don't know how you got through it."

"*How* is that I believe," Esteban said. "Mother Mary got me through. If you believe, you can get through anything."

"Shall we take a walk?" I untied Dalí, and we went down the private road behind our house.

Esteban said, "Anna, I have good news. I have money saved for a trip home I planned for Christmas, but now Ramón will sell me a green card. Because I am not rolling in *dolares*, he will not charge me what he charges others."

"You can buy a green card, E.E.?"

"I told you. I bought my driver's license from him."

"What are they? Forgeries?"

Esteban shrugged. "They are better than nothing," he said. "I am lucky Ramón will not charge me full price."

Dalí was rolling in a field, and I knew what he'd smell like later. Larkin would have to get out the M from The Body Shop and spray it on him. She swore it took away the stench on Dalí, but nothing really did.

"I don't think I like Ramón," I said.

"You don't have to like him. I used to respect him very much, but that was my bad. Now I see he is wrong about many things. He is wrong about you, and I believe he is wrong about Mitzi Graney."

"Ramón doesn't even know me," I said. "What's wrong with Mitzi?"

"Ramón teaches that white females may have disease. Whoever becomes a Blood Brother cannot date a white. Before Virgil took the oath, he worried that your girl friend might have been a run-around, promiss, promisc—"

"Promiscuous?"

"Yes. Playing around with many."

"He's no judge of character, your friend Virgil.

Mitzi was never promiscuous. And I suppose he *wasn't* promiscuous before he met Mitzi?"

"He wasn't. He had his sweethearts at home, but girls we know there do not allow that. Ramón teaches that any *gringuita* over the age of fourteen has probably had sex of some kind. He believes most white girls are *gatas salvajes*, wild cats, loose women."

"That's so not true, E.E.! Do you think I'm a loose woman? Do you think Mitzi Graney is?"

"Ramón teaches that you never know, but he is probably wrong."

I said, "Probably?"

We walked along silently for a while. I thought of times I'd tried to seduce him, how he'd resisted, and I wondered if he thought I always did that with boys.

I asked him, "Why didn't you tell me this before?"

"The wine energizes the tongue, sweet Anna."

I thought of Esteban's hands holding mine so many times, stopping us when we were making out.

"Don't 'sweet Anna' me! So *that's* what stopped you?"

"You might have loved that fellow called Trip. Mitzi told Virgil you were Trip's *amor* last summer."

"We never had sex, Esteban!"

"When I was under Ramón's spell, I wondered about you. But I have seen Ramón make bads about people. He is hard on Chino. He now says the devil controls Chino because Chino won't become a Blood Brother."

"So Ramón was controlling *you*, and maybe still is where we're concerned."

Esteban took my hand. "No. I grew away from him, but he was never the true reason. No other person could tell me to keep away from you. I am not a sheep like Virgil. Anna, what I feared was if you had been experienced, you would see I was not."

"And you think I am?"

He went right on with what he was saying. "I have been with only one girl for such a purpose back home. She was a friend of Gioconda and I was unable. That made me afraid also."

"And I have been with zero boys that way. We're two virgins," I said. "I used to wonder why I wasn't hot for most guys, and then after we met I wondered why you kept stopping us from doing anything. I wondered what was wrong."

"There is something of another nature wrong with me now. Anna, do you know where I will sleep from now on?"

"At Casa Pentecostal?"

"I try to tell you that we can't stay there. The pastor can't harbor illegals and still qualify for a tax-free status. No. As of tomorrow I sleep in a bed another of us sleeps in from eight A.M. until four P.M. I am now a hotbedder. I have half a bureau drawer for my clothes and a corner in the packed closet."

"Where is Gioconda staying, and the others?"

"I waited for them, but they did not wait for me. They went ahead and took a place too small. Sometimes I am like the dog whose bark has been removed. I am macho, and smart, Anna, but it is hard for me to show it."

"I know you're smart."

"Tonight no one did. I am the dummy saying nothing at the table. Then your father asks where do you boys live? Do you pay rent?"

"Sometimes Dad doesn't think."

"He thinks. He's out to get me, Anna!"

"But he didn't get you, Esteban! When you said you didn't have any uncertainties you couldn't handle, you put him in his place."

"Why do I have to put him in his place? Did anyone else there have to put him in his place? He does not treat me like a dinner guest. He treats me like some hood rat who somehow got into his house."

"What's a hood rat? I never heard that before."

"A punk, a street character. A hood rat tries to be serious about wanting to be buried in a casket, because there are worms in the soil, and worse—maggots, though maggots would not be something to say at the dinner table." Esteban was talking so fast, I had to strain to hear him. "But your *padre*—he doesn't care what *he* says at his own table if a hood rat expresses an opinion.

He answers him singing the song about the worms crawling in and out."

"Oh, E.E., calm down. Don't let my father get under your skin that way. He's already forgotten the conversation."

"I am the dummy saying nothing at the table. Then your father asks where do you boys live? Do you pay rent?"

"Shhhh. Hush. Let's not talk about my father."

"He won't go away. He will always be there looking down on me. He is a friend of Charlie Annan, who calls us 'brown bugs.' That's what he calls us, like we're *cucarachas*."

"Okay. Gioconda calls me 'white whore.' Does that make me a white whore?"

"No. But I have to be a man, Anna! If we are to have a future, I have to be a man as you become this college woman."

Right at that moment Dad's old truck came rattling down the driveway, kicking up the gravel, wheels squealing the way they always did when he was in a hurry or mad at something or both.

TWENTY-THREE

WE HURRIED BACK inside the house, where Larkin was rinsing dishes and putting them into the dishwasher.

"Where did Dad go?" I asked her.

"Someone just called to tell Kenny that Charlie Annan is having a secret meeting at the American Legion Hall," she said, "and guess what it's about—that hiring hall your father supports."

"Why doesn't Daddy just stay out of things Charlie Annan cooks up?"

Larkin said, "Because the hiring hall is important to Kenny. Charlie Annan is also planning to go after the contractors who hire illegal immigrants. It's against the law, you know."

She glanced at Esteban quickly, then looked away as though she wasn't sure it was okay to talk about it. Esteban excused himself and went to the bathroom.

Larkin said, "Your brother and Maxine went into the house to watch football."

At least we were spared a ball game on Dad's giant screen.

I said, "Are you *sure* that's why Dad left, Larkin?"

"Of course I'm sure."

"Sometimes when he's angry, he runs away. Goes for walks or drives. You know how he gets quiet when he's steaming inside? Maybe this whole plan backfired on me, and he's mad because I'm seeing Esteban."

"Annabel, I know what he's mad at. He's mad at Charlie Annan. Charlie is going to put your dad out of business if he keeps going."

Dalí smelled so strongly of whatever he'd rolled in that I thought of putting Vicks up my nose to stop the odor, but I didn't think Vicks VapoRub would be very romantic later.

"Maybe he isn't mad about Esteban," I said. "Dad was relatively calm about Esteban being here. He was a little sarcastic, but I'd say he was calm."

"Oh, honey, your daddy is *tired*. He's worn out! He's not calm, he's exhausted!"

"He doesn't usually run off to meetings where he wasn't asked," I said. "That isn't like him at all."

"It isn't like Charlie Annan to turn on him either. They're old friends. How do you think Kenyon got that plush job?"

"Don't ever tell *him* that."

"Let's just relax now until your father gets home," said Larkin, tying the dish towel to the door of the refrigerator. "Do you know what I brought with me? A superb movie we three will love. Particularly Esteban. Part of the reason I picked it is it was filmed in his country."

"In Colombia? What is this film?"

"*Maria Full of Grace.* Kenny would have liked it too, poor man, who never does anything anymore but work! The actress is Kenny's type." She walked down to the end of the screening room, fidgeting with the DVD player. She finally got it ready by the time Esteban reappeared. "I think Kenny likes Latino women," she said. "I know he is mad for Jennifer Lopez."

"Jennifer Lopez was born in the Bronx of New York."

"I didn't know that, Esteban," said Larkin.

I waited for him to say that we'd seen the movie, that it was filmed in Ecuador, not Colombia. Instead, he shot me a look and shook his head as if to tell me not to say anything.

"Catalina Sandino Moreno was the first actress to be nominated for an Oscar for a movie spoken entirely in Spanish," Larkin said. "But don't worry, Annabel, it has English subtitles for us."

Esteban said, "What is someone called who speaks three languages?"

"Trilingual," Larkin said.

"Two languages?"

"Bilingual," said Larkin.

"One language?"

"What?" Larkin asked.

"American," he said.

We all laughed. It wasn't the kind of joke I'd ever heard Esteban tell. I figured he was more PO'ed than he'd told me on our walk. Dad had gotten to him, for sure.

Esteban said, "It's a joke my *vatos* tell. It's not that funny."

Larkin said, "It's funny and it's true."

I made myself an iced tea and asked Esteban what he wanted to drink.

"More sangria, thank you. I never had it before."

Larkin said, "I thought it is what you drink with paella."

"It should be if it isn't," said Esteban. "Very tasty, Missus."

"No, call me Larkin. That's what everyone calls me. I'm not a Mrs. anymore. My husband

and I divorced five years ago."

"Do you have *familia*?"

"If you mean children, no."

"That is a great pity."

"I don't think so. I have my Dalí. When he gets just of the age a son would be ready for college, Dalí will be off to doggy heaven, which doesn't cost a thing."

I couldn't remember Larkin ever talking much about her past. But then I couldn't remember ever asking her about her life, either. All I could remember was that she wanted to go to UCLA and her father was afraid that would result in her marrying a Californian. Since Esteban had come into my life, my world was narrowing down to just the two of us. I wondered what it would be like in a few weeks when school started.

We four settled back on the couch, Dalí beside Larkin.

I was still uneasy about Dad's just taking off like that to go to a meeting. It was hard to believe, even though Larkin seemed to accept it without question.

I thought it could be his way of showing what he thought of my little dinner party, not bothering to even stay for dessert. The strawberry-rhubarb pie I'd bought was sitting on the kitchen counter, two pieces carved out of it. It was Kenyon's favorite, so I knew he and Maxine were eating it watching the game.

I wondered how much time Esteban and I would have at evening's end, and if we could go for a drive, or another walk—someplace we could be alone. When Kenyon took Maxine back to his apartment, Esteban and I could go inside to my room and listen to Shakira. I wanted to talk more about Ramón, too. I wanted to know if Esteban knew that Virgil asked Mitzi to get tested for AIDS. I wanted to know more about Ramón's influence on Esteban, how much of it was still there.

Esteban had always insisted he wanted our first time together to be as perfect as we could make it. He didn't want us to be whipped by sand and wind down on the beach, or somewhere we could be interrupted or found out. He said he wanted us to always have it right, or it could go away. He had even started a song about it: something he called "Don't Be My Summer." "Someone like summer, someone in sun, June July August, over and done? Don't be my summer, be my all year."

He was trying to find an ending for it. He had actually written it in English, but then he switched to Spanish, saying it was more intense in Spanish. In Spanish it worked better if the lyrics just went "You're someone like summer, somcone in sun, June, July, August, over and done? . . ." He said he would have to work on it until it was right.

"Why not just leave it in English?" I'd asked him.

"Because the English is wrong for it."

"I like it, though."

"But I have to sing it, and it has not the same melancholy it has in my own language."

"Why do you like melancholy so much?" I'd asked him.

"It's the heart of life's stories, Anna. Great songs don't celebrate joy unless they are parade marches."

I hadn't liked *Maria Full of Grace* that much when I first saw it, and as I watched it in the screening room, I tried to dismiss the plot and concentrate on the Spanish. That didn't last long. The actors spoke too fast. I thought again about taking Spanish as a second language. In the fall, when the tourists left our town, there were always advertisements on supermarket billboards for SSL classes. The high school offered one too, but Dad would probably attend that one, since it was a night class, popular with businesspeople.

Every time the thought of SSL came into my head, it had a path that led to a fantasy future when I would be in Esteban's homeland, meeting his family. I already knew that besides his mother, stepfather, and Gioconda there were his twin sisters, another sister, and his two brothers. Esteban had mentioned several times that his father had suddenly disappeared, just as

Chino's brother had.

Sometimes I tried to imagine myself living in Providencia with Esteban. I knew that was where he wanted to live his life. I didn't know if I could bear to be that far from the United States. When I thought about it, I'd tell myself, *Slow down, Anna B. Put it in the Put It Off file.* But you can't stop yourself from daydreaming, from imagining a future with someone you love, no matter how unlikely it seems. I had never really been in love before. I didn't know what I was willing to risk, or even if I *was* ready to risk at all. Since I'd met Esteban, I didn't think any further ahead than graduation from high school. Now suddenly it began to register what it meant that Esteban was undocumented. I could lose him without doing anything to cause it. One day I could turn around and he'd be gone.

When the phone rang, Larkin pushed PAUSE on the remote and said, "I hope it's Kenny."

Esteban excused himself and went into the bathroom again.

* * *

I looked up at the nails coming through the roof and I thought of that night. It was my most frequent, hot daydream. I'd go over and over Esteban loving me for the first time, looking at me with those serious brown eyes, bringing his lips to mine, our bodies pressed together. I'd felt as though we both had wings. Then I remember him shouting *"Basta!"* Next came the trip to get the paella and then the very couch I was sitting on, I was lying on with the Swan Man. It was the beginning of becoming a woman, of feeling finally what the songs and poems said you felt. Before Esteban, I'd thought all the words like *swooning*, *rapture*, *thrill*, *tremble* were *hyperbole*. My mother's favorite word. The times Dad used to dream of putting the family in a trailer and going off to see the USofA, taking our sweet time, maybe being gone for years, I'd say, "What about school?" Mom would whisper in my ear, "Shhhh. It's Daddy dreaming, Annabel. It's just hyperbole."

"No! No!" Larkin cried out, her voice so shrill, Dalí jumped down from the couch and went toward her.

When she closed her cell, she said, "Get your brother, Annabel. Kenny's in Seaview Hospital. He's had a heart attack."

The plan was for Larkin to drive to the hospital immediately with Kenyon and Maxine. Esteban and I would meet them there, after I let Dalí out a last time, turned off the lights, the stove, the TV—made sure the house wouldn't go up in flames and Dalí wouldn't get cramps from holding it. One of Mom's rules had always been never to leave a house in a hurry; be sure it would be there when you headed home again.

We were still in the driveway when Esteban turned off the motor and shook his head.

"*Coño!* Anna, I can't go there."

"Yes, you can. Why can't you?"

"It's impossible."

"Charlie Annan won't be there, if that's the reason. And even if he is, I *have* to be there! You can just go on! It's my dad, E.E.! It's—"

He cut me off. "I can't *drive*! I can't see right."

"What do you mean?"

225

"The wine. I now see two roads and four trees."

"Oh my God, are you seeing double?"

"*Sí. Sí.* You will have to drive."

"I can't drive, E.E.! I never learned!"

"If *policía* arrest me drunk, that would be big trouble for me. I have no residence, and my driver's license is the Ridge Road address. There would be questions."

"Esteban, you don't sound drunk. I didn't see you stagger!"

"There is no argument here. I cannot walk the straight line. I cannot drive. I did not know the wine would make my eyes go *loco*."

"Then I have to call a taxi!" I said.

"I'm sorry, Anna."

"So am I! How could you get drunk?"

We got out of the Pontiac, and he said, "I can go there with you in the taxi. I am not that drunk."

But inside the screening room, while he waited for me to telephone Seaview Ride, he fell asleep on the couch, the nails coming through

226

the roof above him. Sticking out of his back pocket was a small envelope with a blue ribbon on it.

On the outside he had written: "For Anna to see because she wanted to. xxEE."

I left him sleeping there.

I opened the envelope in the backseat of the taxi. There were four photographs. I knew they were the pictures of his family that he had promised me he'd send for. I couldn't deal with that then. All I could do was put them in my bag and ask the driver to hurry.

"Please stop saying that, lady," he finally said. "I'm going too fast as it is."

So am I, I thought. What if something happened to my father? With everything else he was handling, he had to come home that night and discover I'd gone against his rules, gone behind his back to date someone he didn't know, and didn't know anything about. He'd probably guessed Esteban was an illegal. Then he must have known I had fallen hard for him too, because never in my life had I disobeyed him in such a major way. Who could blame him for worrying about what I was capable of under those circumstances? He'd already had a major loss he was just beginning to recover from with Larkin. Now there was me to worry about, when I'd *never* given him any big problem. I was always his good girl.

They were operating on Dad when I got to the hospital—emergency bypass. We walked and waited and drank coffee and waited. While everyone was down in the cafeteria getting something to eat, I looked at the photographs Esteban had gotten for me.

One was of a large woman, taller than Esteban, with her arm around him while he looked up at her, smiling. He seemed very young, but there was no mistaking Esteban. On the back he had written, "Mi madre and me."

There was a photo of a young woman carrying a baby, seated with twin women holding a set of twins on their laps, "My sister Pilar and her daughter with my twin sisters Nadia and Nilce, and Nadia's twin boys."

The third photograph showed his brothers Jorge and Alejandro, seven or eight years old, playing catch with his stepfather.

At first I thought the last picture was Esteban again. Then I noticed the clothes were old, and this man had a tiny mustache. He wore one gold hoop earring. On the back, Esteban had written "Hugolino Santiago, last seen in Providencia July 8, 1991."

I thought of my own father, of the chance I would never see him again, and I wished I could pray, or believe in anything.

TWENTY-FOUR

M Y DAD WAS RECOVERING from his bypass at Larkin's. The very next day after he went to Seaview Hospital, I'd left a message on Esteban's voice mail that I wanted to see him. I asked him to please forgive me for making him go through such an evening.

I didn't know how Esteban got wherever he was going from our house. His old Pontiac was still in our driveway. As long as it was there, I had the hope of seeing him. I was beginning to lose hope of getting through to him.

If I had been thinking of Esteban instead of myself, I would have known my father would never accept him, for exactly the reason both Larkin and Kenyon had told me. Dad was terrified of losing me. Losing my mother had been hard enough.

All right. I would not be the first daughter who'd disappointed her father by falling in love with the wrong fellow. I was certainly not the first girl to have a boyfriend who'd never measure up in a parent's eyes. And as much as Esteban was bent on measuring up, he'd just have to go without Dad's okay. What I should have done from the beginning was level with Dad: tell him if he really did want me to be part of the family, he had to accept Esteban and me as a couple. We'd follow his rules about curfews and other dating behavior, but he mustn't forbid us to see each other. If he did that, we'd only see each other behind his back. Nobody would be happy that way.

I had gone to Seaview Jewelry and bought a pair of gold hoop earrings. I would wear one hoop and one would be Esteban's. There went my school clothes budget I'd begun saving for that summer.

It was about time *I* was the gift giver, and about time I understood Esteban better. He hadn't told me so much of what he'd blurted out after some sangria, and whose fault was that? I could still remember when he'd first mentioned that his father had disappeared one day (he'd snapped his fingers and said, "Like that"). I hadn't asked him anything about it. I'd actually said something sarcastic about Dad, about some-times wishing *he'd* disappear, because I wasn't really hearing Esteban—any more than I was thinking of why he'd muttered at dinner that night something about believing there should be a casket and a burial. Those were two things his father had never had.

At the library I looked for him every time the door opened, and trashed myself for being angry with him because he'd gotten wasted. When I ran through the conversation while eating paella (did anyone compliment him on how good it was?), I could see the whole evening through Esteban's eyes. I could remember him unpacking the paella and complaining "Don't you even listen?" Who wouldn't get soused?

Wednesday evening he wasn't at the soccer field, which was major! Since I'd known him, he'd never missed a game. None of his old Ridge Road *vatos* played in that game. There was no one I could ask about him. But that night as I bicycled up my driveway, I saw Dario and Virgil standing by Esteban's Pontiac.

They waved at me, Dario with a big smile, Virgil frowning, probably imagining someone with an STD, herpes, or HIV waving back. Like so many two-faced characters, he had his hand out to shake mine and a look of innocence in his brown eyes.

Just Tuesday night Mitzi had called to tell me all was well. She had told her mother everything. They had gone to the family doctor and she was okay. As for Virgil? She said she'd get over him. She'd help me get over Esteban when I needed her. She said, "And you will, Annabel."

"I don't want to get over Esteban," I told her.

"Not now," she said.

Esteban's *vatos* were leaning against his car.

"We didn't want to just drive off in Teban's car," Dario said, "or you would think it was being stolen."

"How are you guys?"

"Fine! Great!" they both chorused.

"How did Esteban get home Saturday night?"

"I drove here to get him," Dario said.

"And where is Esteban?"

"Away," Dario said.

"He didn't tell me he was going away. Where did he go?"

Dario took a letter from his back pocket. "He has written to you all about where he goes."

Virgil said, "He gave us the key to the car."

"He gave us the car," said Dario.

"To use while he's away?"

"Yes," Dario said. "To use. We have a new place to live far from Dr. Annan."

"Very far," Virgil said. "Far and high. We are

in an attic. I like that because the train whistle sounds late at night."

"Is Esteban okay?"

"He is okay," Virgil said.

"Where is he?" I looked him right in the eyes, but if he knew Mitzi and Esteban had told me all about his suspicious ways, he was a good con man. He only smiled, sounding cheerful as he said, "His letter will say where he is."

"Tell your father we are sorry for his health," Dario said. "Tell him we work extra hard so he won't lose money."

They got into the Pontiac, and I waited until they were gone before I opened the letter.

My dear Anna,

I am so glad to be told by Mitzi your father goes home from the hospital and is okay. I asked her to call you and report back, for I am so ashamed I cannot even go to the library.

If things had gone in a bad way for your father, I would not have wished it. In the sober light I see that he is right. Maybe I am no hood rat, but I am no son-in-law material as well. I do not blame him for not wanting me around you.

When I come to your house, I had an envelope with me where inside were photographs of my family. If you have not found it, look for it please (there is a blue ribbon around it) because I want you to have those. You told me once you would like to see my familia. *Maybe you were just being polite, but I still want you to see them even if you will probably never meet them at all.*

Anna, in our house in Providencia there are photographs so there is no wall space. They are all of familia, *and if you think your father is strict on who dates his daughter, you should meet my stepfather and my mother, for they are so particular about who joins the* familia.

I have thought so much about them since this is happening. We were never one of money. None of us growing up expected yes we would go to university or college as yours does and your friends. I think it is the cause we are poor, and some come to America to send back money. If no one breaks away from that habit, then we are in for the shame like I now face being a hotbedder, being not fit to date some man's daughter. I see life on the other side of that and I wish it not just for me, but for my own familia.

I have thought and thought about Ramón's offer to sell me a green card, and I believe it would be another bad, for what if I got caught? I would go from bad to the worst, jail perhaps. Perhaps I would be shipped back and then of no good to anyone.

But Chino has given me a new idea. When we found him at last, he said a policeman almost arrested him for sleeping on the beach but instead sat down and talked to him about how to become legal, how to be a man who matters in this world.

Anna, amante, Chino and I will become soldiers in the United States Army. Anna, by doing that, I can not only get a green card eventually, but this would be my chance for money and for myself to attend college.

There is a saying we have: "Do not be like them, be better than them. Then you will get someplace." I have never paid mind to that because how could I be better? Now I see a way.

Joining the United States Army would give me the tools. Money. College. The rest would be up to me. I want to be like others and better than others, too, and this is now my goal.

I go with Chino to join up tomorrow, Anna, the very day you read this. I am told I will learn everything, even how to work a computer. So maybe I can send an e-mail to you one day and find out what you are doing, if you choose to answer. Not right *away, dear Anna, but sometimes off in the future.*

I cannot take the chance to see you before I go. I cannot face your disapproval if that is your feeling since I was too drunk to be there for an emergency. Neither could I face your forgiveness. It would only remind me of all the times you would have to forgive me until I became educated and mature.

I love you, Anna, but I do not love you more than my pride, my manhood, my wish to be a responsible person. I cannot ask you to be mine, and even as I am changing, I would not ask you to promise me anything meanwhile.

I knew when I met you that you would change my life. The hard part is I did not think of that life without you. Losing my lucky medal began my down the hill. God was telling me something maybe that I was not enough for someone like you. "Dare to Forget Me"? Please do forget me, Anna. Let me think of you deciding which college would be best and getting back with your Seaview girl friends, going on with what you would have done anyway if you had never met Esteban Santiago.

P.S. Dear Anna, please play Shakira. I wish we could listen together to all of them, but please listen to "Whenever, Wherever." Not to read any message from me in that song, but some of it will have memories of us. I do not think it is a bad to have sweet memories when you have nothing more of each other. Memories are better than nothing, and memories of you, my love, are my gold. Good-bye, God bless even if you don't want Him to bless you, I pray He will do it.

E.E.

TWENTY-FIVE

MY DEAREST, *loco, lovely,* amor, *my Esteban,*

This is the sixth letter I've written you, then ripped up because I cannot seem to find the right words to say don't do this, good-bye, stay safe, don't go, I love you so!

I am so sorry about that embarrassing, humiliating dinner party I inflicted on you. I should have known better. We have a saying that you cannot make a silk purse out of a sow's ear, and neither can you make a gracious, kind father out of Dad, who sees you as this threat to our boring life here in Seaview. Esteban, my father never saw you as a hood rat. He never saw you as someone inferior. He would not have been so frightened of you if that was all he saw. You are from another land and another culture, and the idea of my going there with you was what he feared. I wonder now if he wasn't right about that, for I was always aware that you wanted to go home and live with your family close.

Now that Larkin has come into my father's life, I don't think of him as a lonely man anymore. Kenyon has his girlfriend, and Kenyon will probably always live near Seaview. I would be the one willing to try a change. Dad knows that.

But this doesn't make any sense now, does it? There is no point now to my saying I'm sorry for what I've done, or to my saying I suspect I would have gone with you to Providencia one day, if you had asked me to.

Now all I can say that does make sense is please, please watch out. Take care of yourself the best that you can.

There is no point either in my telling you I hate this war, for no one going to it really wants to put him- or herself in such terrible danger! But whenever I hear or see anything about Iraq, I remember Dad helping this veteran a little younger than my brother. He came home blind, minus a leg. That was the first time I ever thought about war at all. After that I wouldn't watch when Iraq came on the TV news. I always remembered Dad talking of this vet's "courage," and I'd ask myself which would you rather have—courage or your right leg? Oh sweet, sweet Swan Man, please try not to prove you are as good as or better than anyone. Try not to be a hero!

Esteban, my e-mail address is AnnaB@ aol.com. You know my snail mail address.

One day I hope you will use either one to tell me yours, to tell me you're all right, to tell me whatever you feel I should know, or whatever you feel like saying.

I will never, ever forget you, Swan Man. We do have many good memories and many are view memories. Remember when you told me that we should visit places with wonderful scenery so when we looked back we would have it there to enjoy?

I am enclosing here a gold earring. I hope you won't think it's nervy of me to send you something like the earring I saw your father wore in the photograph. I remembered, too, you mentioning that once to me, that he wore one in his ear. You will have to get your ear pierced, as both of mine are. (It will not hurt you, Swan Man. It will only look that way.) And I am right now wearing the match to the one enclosed for you.

Oh, Esteban, watch your every step. Don't take chances or volunteer for dangerous missions. Write me someday, please? I love you. I will never forget you, even if you forget me, because you are the first one who ever made me feel like a woman. I love you so, mi amor, *I can't say good-bye.*

Anna

TWENTY-SIX

CHARLIE ANNAN'S WHITE Saab convertible was parked outside of Feelfree when Kenyon and I arrived. Feelfree was the name of Larkin's house overlooking Accabonac Bay. She had decided to have Dad recuperate there. On a Sunday noon in late August Kenyon drove me to see them, after he went to church.

I groaned when I saw Charlie's car, and Kenyon said, "Remember, Anna B., I work for the guy."

"I know."

"He doesn't know about you and Esteban, so if you act cool to him, he won't know why. He'll think you blame him for what happened to Dad."

"He was part of the reason for Dad's heart attack, wasn't he? He wanted to have that meeting behind Dad's back."

"Annabel, we butt out when it comes to their politics. Dad and Charlie have had their disagreements before. Their friendship has always survived their differences. Charlie's very upset about Dad. He's been on the phone to Larkin three or four times a day."

"What does Dad say about him?"

"They're old buddies, Annabel. This isn't going to come between them. You know that."

I hadn't yet told Kenyon or Dad anything about Esteban's letter or his plan to join the army. Only Larkin knew, and Mitzi.

I was glad Larkin had taken Dad to her house, because he would have known something was wrong if I'd been around him for very long.

I had finally stopped crying, and I'd also given up the idea I could change anything.

Larkin offered Kenyon and me iced tea, which Dr. Annan was drinking while Dalí smelled his shoes.

"Annabel," said Dr. Annan, "I hope you appreciate the fact there's nothing personal in any of this."

"I know for you there isn't," I said, feeling tears behind my eyes. Kenyon shot me a look as though he was afraid I'd lose it.

"Ken and I have disagreed on a lot of things," said the doctor, "but we stay friends."

Dad's voice: "We don't have any choice," laughing, as he appeared in his old sweats with a BROWN AROUND TOWN T, his white socks and sandals.

Charlie Annan made room for Dad on the couch, and Kenyon sat on the leather hassock near them.

"Annabel, do you want to go into my studio and critique my art?"

"Oh, I'd love that, Larkin."

She knew I wanted to get away from Charlie. She knew everything, even about the night I locked Esteban and myself out of Kenyon's apartment. At the hospital, waiting for news of Dad, we'd talked for hours by ourselves.

But as close as we'd become, this was my first visit to her home. That was how estranged I'd been from everyone and everything but Esteban that summer.

Kenyon got up to come to the studio with me, saying he'd like another look himself.

Dad said, "Son? Tell that girlfriend of yours I'm not ready to be put into the hole yet."

Charlie laughed. Kenyon must have told him about Maxine and Green Pastures, or maybe it was nervous laughter.

"Please," said Larkin, "can we talk about life instead of its alternative?"

Dalí joined my brother and me in Larkin's studio.

Around us the walls were filled with Larkin's strange work, which she called environmental

249

art. Her paintings were of birds grounded because of oil on their wings, of deer running from woods where trees were being cut down by power chain saws, and of land and lakes barren and polluted. She had assemblages and collages made of driftwood, beach stones, even recycled plastic bags.

Kenyon shook his head and said, "Dad must *really* love her."

I said, "It's funny about Dad. He attracts very hip women, yet he's so square himself."

"Maybe he's good in the sack."

I made a face. "Yick and yuck! Don't put that picture in my mind."

"How are *you* doing, Sis? You were so quiet coming over here."

That was all he needed to say. I told him everything. I'd cry, get a grip, bear up, then begin all over again.

After, Kenyon was quiet for a minute and then he shook his head sadly and said, "So he's going to be one of those green-card soldiers. I'm sorry to hear that, Anna B. I mean it."

"He could get killed, couldn't he, Kenyon?"

"Of course he could! That's the idea. We're running out of cannon fodder over there."

I began to cry again, and Kenyon said, "I'm sorry. That was a stupid thing for me to say."

"Larkin says the same thing. And she says there's something called the Montgomery GI Bill that promises them not just fifty thousand dollars but postservice employment and training. She says on the internet it says these promises aren't kept."

"You know Larkin. She's always been against that war."

"And you're not, Kenyon?"

"I'm beginning to think I'm like most educated white boys, Anna B. Let the underclass fight for me. But I don't know what the hell they're fighting *for*!"

I said, "They're only following orders. Wasn't that what Hitler's henchmen said?"

"Not just his henchmen. The whole country went along with his agenda." Kenny shook his head. "I hope you get my sarcasm."

"I get it."

"I hope you don't think your big brother is only good for worming cats and putting down old critters. I don't often argue politics, but Larkin's not the only one who can see we're sending the minorities and disenfranchised to the front lines. We have a long tradition of using the poor and uneducated that way."

"Esteban's so sure he can improve himself by doing it," I said.

"With luck, maybe he can, honey."

"What did you really think of him?"

"Really?"

"Yes."

"I think the guy's got iron balls to face up to Dad the way he did. That's for starters." We were sitting in these crazy chairs made out of wagon wheels. "He's a nice boy, Anna, but he *is* a boy. I don't care how old he is. He's a kid. He was doing his best—unskilled work in a strange country, sending what money he could back to his folks. Look, maybe the army *will* make a man of him."

"What would make him a man, Kenyon?"

"Confidence, a skill or an education, a place of his own, and a right to be wherever he is."

"I wonder if I'll ever see him again," I said.

Dalí was panting hard. It was ninety-degree weather, and the air conditioning in Larkin's studio was weak.

Kenyon sighed, stood up, and walked around, looking at Larkin's art on the four walls.

I knew he didn't particularly like it, but anything not to have to reply to what I'd just said.

By the time we left the studio, Charlie had gone.

When I sat down beside Dad, he said, "Glad to be going back to school in a few days, honey?"

"Yes." That was true. I missed myself. I missed all the old familiar friends and routines.

"I know you're a little put out with your old man, Anna B., but that boy has a long way to go."

"He's not a boy."

"Well, he's not a man, either. I'm sorry if you thought I didn't put out the red carpet for him."

"I'm getting over our little dinner party, Dad."

"You've got something bigger to get over, Anna B."

"Dad? I'm dealing with it, okay?"

The night before I received Esteban's letter, I'd finished reading F. Scott Fitzgerald's *The Crackup*. I hadn't known yet that E.E. was gone, but I'd sensed something was changed. I wasn't sure if it was a change in me, or in Esteban, or a change in both of us. I'd taken a bath using the Anna Sui gel. My eyes had filled with tears when I'd read one of Fitzgerald's silly jingles: *"There was an orchestra—Bingo-Bango, playing for us to dance the Tango,"* and I thought of E.E. and me down on the boardwalk with the boom box going, the moonlight bright, and his eyes watching all over my face while we danced.

"I'm coming home tomorrow, honey," Dad said.

"I'll have dinner ready."

"Don't fuss. Some takeout will do."

"*Won't* do," Larkin said. "I'll bring the food. I know your diet, Kenny."

"You know me better than anyone," Dad said. Then he got red, looked at me sheepishly, and said, "No offense, Annabel. I just meant—"

I cut him off as he was struggling to finish the sentence. "No offense taken, Dad. Larkin's been a lifesaver." She was the only person who could have changed how I felt about another woman coming along. The moment she'd come into his life, he hadn't seemed as much like his old self as he did like someone new. I'd never seen him fall in love before, and never seen a woman fall for him, either. After Mom died, I wondered what I'd feel if that ever happened. I didn't think I'd be able to warm up to anyone who'd try to take Mom's place. I hadn't counted on Larkin. I hadn't even thought of a woman who wasn't interested in replacing Mom. Larkin was interested in finding her own place with Dad, and she had.

Maxine had left Seaview after Dad's operation. I was glad of that. One loving couple was enough. I sat there envying Dad and Larkin, and trying to think how I could get the gold earring to Esteban. Somehow I trusted Dario. Dad always had the address of anyone who worked for him, and Dario was a regular, probably because he was documented. I could ask Dario for Esteban's address. It would be like Esteban to warn Dario that I might do that, and forbid him to give it to me. In that case I'd put my letter in a package with the ring, wrap it carefully, get it stamped, and ask Dario to mail it for me.

I wanted to go home and cry some more, in private, listen to Mercedes Solo and Shakira, and try to write Esteban another letter. I wanted to keep the part about staying safe, but I wanted to tell him to shoot himself in the foot—to do something to make it impossible for him to go to Iraq.

I said, "Are you ready to leave, Kenyon?"

"We just got here."

"Don't stay on my account," said Dad. "I have to get on the horn and scrounge around for a new crew. We got the Jamison job, so we're going to have our hands full."

"We'll talk about that," said Larkin. "Annabel, come outside with me a moment. I want to tell you something."

"When do you go back to school?" Dad asked me.

"September seventh," I said.

"Go ahead, you two," Kenyon said. "I want to watch the game soon, anyway, so I'll watch it in the screening room if I'm taking Sis home."

Larkin walked across to the back door and held it open for me.

She said, "No, Dalí!"

Dalí came anyway.

It was hot. It had been the hottest summer I could remember. I'd tried to tell Esteban that when he said our summers were so much like the ones in Colombia. I could see him in his bib overalls, my favorite clothes of his, but I could see him in his cargo shorts, too. I couldn't stop seeing him.

"I'm going to write Esteban," Larkin said, "and tell him he is welcome to return to Seaview and stay on the estate of an artist friend of mine. He needs a groundskeeper. Esteban would make a good salary, and he could work for me, too, help me lift and pack things."

"It's too late, Larkin. He said he would be in the army when I got his letter."

"Things can go wrong. I hope they do."

"Dad would never forgive you if you found work and a home here for Esteban."

"And I will never forgive myself if something happens to that boy. Why didn't I find him a place to live after Charlie got them all booted out? I knew Chet Boterf needed someone to live on the premises."

"Larkin, it's nobody's fault, really."

"It's all of our faults! What are we doing to stop this war?"

Dalí was off in the field rolling around the way he did. Neither Larkin nor I had sat down in the chairs on the terrace there. It was scorching. I had the feeling neither one of us wanted to say much more, anyway. I would start crying and Larkin would get into a rage about the war.

"I'm going home, Larkin. I feel like I've been away when I haven't been anywhere."

"There's one more thing," she said. "Hold out

your hand. Close your eyes."

I waited until I felt something drop into my palm before I looked down.

It was Esteban's gold holy medal.

"I told Charlie that I knew whose it was, and he was only too happy to return it," Larkin said.

"You told Charlie about Esteban and me?"

"I fibbed. No. I *lied*. I said you'd lent Kenyon's apartment to a school friend and her Latino boyfriend. But you gave them the wrong key and they were locked out. I said this boy ran off because he was afraid to get the girl in trouble, and afraid he would be accused of trying to break in."

"And Charlie believed it?"

"Charlie said the boy was probably undocumented, that they were always afraid they'd be arrested. He said he bet you'd never try that again, and that if Kenyon ever found out, there'd be big trouble between you two." She put her arm around me and said, "I didn't even say Esteban's name. I said I didn't know who the boy was, but that he was only there to see his girlfriend, not to steal."

"Dad better watch out. You're a fast thinker."

"No. I'm a slow thinker, but I think hard when I paint. I kept thinking of Esteban without his holy medal. There is something so touching about these young men, so far from their families, up here facing so much hostility. I feel for them. And for you, sweetie. I know what you're going through."

"It's Esteban's lucky piece, too. He'll need it for sure!"

I would send it with the earring and the last letter I'd already written to Esteban. No more redoing letters to him.

Larkin and I hugged, and Dalí came rushing at Larkin to break it up.

"You know, Annabel, your father could stay another week with me, if that would make it easier for you."

"It would make it easier, maybe, but it's time I took some responsibility."

"That's hard when you're deep-down angry with someone."

"Speaking of deep down, don't I know him by

now, Larkin? Remember, I'm not religious, so how come I expected a miracle on paella night? Dad was Dad. He's always going to be the way he is. I'm the one who needs to change."

She said, "Please don't change too much. I like you so, Annabel."

"I like you, too. Dad's lucky."

"Isn't he?" She laughed.

On the way home I told Kenyon how sweet I thought Larkin was to get Charlie to return Esteban's precious keepsake. Kenyon said Dad had just told him he was going to ask Larkin to marry him.

"It's a good thing they don't rehash the paella dinner," I said, "because Larkin agrees with me that Dad humiliated Esteban." Was that even true? I couldn't remember her saying that.

"How about forgetting the paella dinner? I think you just like to say paella so you can feel close to Esteban."

"Paella certainly figured a lot in our relationship."

"Maxine said it was the best paella she'd ever tasted."

"Why didn't she say it at the time?"

"Round and round we go," Kenyon said, "and where we stop is where we started. The f-ing paella dinner."

"Sorry."

"I know you can't help it."

"How about some music?" I said.

"I haven't heard any news all day, either," my brother said. Then he said, "Sis? I know it sounds corny, but this, too, will pass."

"There's a part of me that knows that. The same part that knows I probably won't see him again."

Kenyon turned the radio on.

We rode along listening to reports of a hurricane named Katrina.

"Forecasters fear that storm-driven waters will lap over the New Orleans levees when monster Hurricane Katrina pushes past the Crescent City tomorrow."

"It sounds like a big one!" Kenyon said.

"Why do people live down there? Why do people live where there are hurricanes and floods, year after year? Why don't they move?"

Kenny said, "Because that's where they live. That's where their roots are. And everyone they care about."

"Familia," I said.

Kenyon glanced over at me, smiling, brushing back a lock of my hair.

He said, "Yes. Family."

Los Gatos High School